Lure *of the* Outlands

KEITH KELTNER

Contents

❋

Dedication

She graduated from St. Agnes Academy in 1940 and always held a great admiration and respect for her alma mater. While she was a student there, she learned of the dedication and sacrifice of the nuns as they cared for the yellow fever victims of Memphis. Over the following years, she amassed volumes of notes and research in hope that one day she would write a story about the yellow fever epidemics that gripped the city. Unfortunately, various life events interfered with her plans and she died before writing her story. With her research lost over the years, I was left with only my love for her to guide my journey to write this story. I'll never know the story she wanted to tell and I can only pray that she would have approved of my attempt to honor those who stayed in Memphis while all the others fled. This story is dedicated to my mother, Margaret Belote.

Chapter One

The Snow King

"I'm telling you, the Krewe of Rex Parade was delayed while snow was removed from the route!"

"Doc, you don't know what you're talking about! It never snows back home."

"Not only did it snow, the temperatures dropped down to only five degrees. They say it's the coldest Fat Tuesday New Orleans has ever had."

After glancing over the patient's medical chart, the doctor continued. "Didn't you see the newspaper? It's snowing all the way down to Tampa. They are having blizzards along the Florida Gulf Coast. Folks can't remember a colder winter."

"I still say you're trying to fool me, doc!"

"I'm not trying to fool you! Now, please excuse me; I need to talk with the head nurse for a minute."

As the doctor walked away, the New Orleans native just sneered as he adjusted his arm sling and mumbled, "It never snows back home!"

Walking towards the head nurse, the doctor made a couple of stops to quickly check on a couple of other patients who were awake. Approaching the nurse, he asked, "Where is Cuz?"

"Good morning, Dr. Hodge. Cuz was making another one of his scenes so we moved him so that he wouldn't bother the other patients."

The nurse and Dr. Hodge discussed the effects malaria was having on the patient known as Cuz. Once the fever climbs to a certain point, the brain starts to play tricks on a person. In this case, Cuz had restless nights punctuated with vivid nightmares and verbal outbursts. Many times after waking, Cuz would not remember these nightmares and would only comment on how wet his clothing and sheets were from his sweat.

"Doctor, he screamed out that he had killed somebody named Stumpy."

"That's the third time, isn't it?"

The nurse nodded. "I thought most malaria-related nightmares weren't so vivid. Do you think he really did murder some guy named Stumpy or is his mind just remembering some story he's heard?"

"Fortunately, I'm just an Army doctor responsible for treating his wounds and burns. If he did murder someone, I'm sure that's a matter for the police to figure out. As for Cuz losing his mind, well, why don't we just focus on healing his body before we cart him off to an asylum. Agreed?"

The nurse laughed as she agreed.

Following the nurse's directions, Doctor Hodge located Cuz and found that he was staring at the corner of the room with a glazed expression. "Good morning, Cuz. How are you doing today?"

Shocked back to reality, he fidgeted with his sheets slightly as he replied, "Yes, sir, captain. It's a fine day."

The doctor examined the scars from the multiple wounds and burns Cuz had on his arms, chest, left leg, and foot "Are you still having problems putting your weight on your left foot?"

"Yes, sir, captain. It hurts like a... Well, sir, it still hurts plenty."

The doctor gestured towards the burned area on his patient and said, "Those burns are healing faster than we expected. As soon as we're able to fix that foot of yours, we should be able to send you home."

Cuz forced a smile as he glanced away. After a brief pause, he asked the doctor, "What about this malaria sickness? Will I have it forever like the old timers in the regiment were saying?"

"First, we'll keep you on the quinine treatments since it seems to be the most effective way of dealing with the sickness. Next, I will tell you that there is a lot about malaria that we don't know. Many believe that it is spread by mosquitoes in the same way we think that yellow fever is spread. There have been cases when we cured someone with the quinine treatments who then showed signs of getting it again months later. Now, is the quinine just a temporary cure, or are these victims getting bit by infected mosquitoes again? We just don't have all of the answers yet. But I can tell you that the Army has really good men working on this problem. Just last month I met a fellow Army doctor by the name of Walter Reed who is working diligently on this very issue. If anyone can find a cure, I have to believe it will be an Army doctor and perhaps this Walter Reed character himself."

Cuz's reaction confused the doctor. He thought the prospect of being released within a couple of weeks would have caused a happier reaction. After making a couple of notes in the patient's medical record, the doctor asked, "Is there something troubling you I should know about?"

Cuz again forced a brief smile while responding, "I guess I'll be all right as long as I don't drown in my own sweat from these fever episodes."

"As the medicine takes effect, you should have less fever. I almost forgot; Major Weitz will be here to see you this afternoon."

"Major Weitz? He's coming here to see me? Why? Why would he come here?"

Doctor Hodge laughed slightly as he replied, "My guess is that he is visiting men under his command who are in the hospital."

In a muffled response, Cuz said, "I think I would've liked it better if he visited us more often in the trenches."

"I take it that you are not looking forward to your commanding officer's visit?"

"Hell, no..." Cuz stopped as he composed himself. He fidgeted slightly before continuing, "I mean, sir, Major Weitz ain't my commanding officer. That'd be Captain Washington. He was right there with us all the way! Colonel Carrol led us and the rest of the Sixth Cavalry there in Cuba. We saw some of him in the fighting too. Major Weitz, well, sir, I don't know what he was supposed to be doing, but we never saw much of him when the lead started flying."

"I see," replied the doctor. After a pause and a small shrug, he stated, "Well, Cuz, I have no clue as to why the major is coming here then. I guess you'll find out this afternoon."

After a restless morning filled with wild curiosity, Cuz heard the brisk approach of footsteps. Turning to see, he noticed Major Weitz and his doctor, Captain Hodge, rapidly walking towards him.

Squirming in his bed in an effort to sit up straighter and render a salute, Cuz was unprepared for the strange smile on the two men's faces. The suspense was terrible for him. He was growing more nervous by the second. Was it the simple curiosity about the unexpected visit? Was it the malaria kicking in? Maybe it was some reaction to the quinine for which he was unprepared.

Major Weitz spoke first. "Sergeant Gunsie Hayes, it is my honor to inform you that Captain A.B. Washington, Commanding Officer of D Troop, of the Sixth Cavalry, has recommended you to receive the Medal of Honor for your actions while under heavy enemy fire in Cuba."

Cuz just sat there with a blank stare on his face as he tried to comprehend what he had just heard. In a faint whisper, it sounded as if he just uttered, "...no..."

Captain Hodge interjected, "This is certainly a great honor, Cuz. I had no idea as to the events that contributed to your earlier injuries. I was also unaware of the fact that you were personally responsible for saving 15 fellow soldiers. From what the major tells me, you are quite deserving of this award."

The two officers gave Cuz a moment to absorb the news. The major then said, "The recommendation has already been approved by Colonel Carroll, but will still need to go through a couple of more approvals before..."

Cuz then interrupted the major with a defiant, "No, sir!"

The major was momentarily caught off guard by such an insolent response as he glanced towards the doctor for some possible explanation.

Meanwhile, the captain studied Cuz's expression for any sign as to what caused such an outburst. He then asked Cuz, "Do you understand that you are being awarded the Medal of Honor?"

Cuz's face became more determined. "No, sir! You can't do that! I didn't do it for a medal. I tell you, I don't want the award. Stop telling people about this. No, I don't want it. Do you hear me? I don't want it!"

The longer Cuz went on, the redder his face became. Tears began streaming down his cheeks mixing with the rapidly appearing beads of sweat. Cuz's rant started changing into confusing gibberish, which left both officers shocked and puzzled. At one point, Cuz blurted, "Wasn't 15 years of fighting enough? Why are y'awl still trying to kill me for what happened to Stumpy?"

When the nurse approached to try to calm him, Cuz responded by grabbing her and telling the men to give the medal to her. She continued to work on calming him down as the two officers stepped away.

"Well, that's not exactly the reaction I'd expected."

The doctor replied, "It may be the malaria. He's been struggling with delusions whenever his fever shoots up. I'm sure he'll look at things differently after his next quinine treatment. Once he's stable, I'll talk to him about it."

The major glanced back towards Cuz as he told the doctor, "All I know is that the colonel sees what the sergeant there did back in Cuba as being extraordinary and deserving of this nation's highest possible recognition. It's my job to see that he gets it." He then looked the captain in the eye and said, "Doctor, it's your job to make sure he accepts it!"

The doctor started to protest. "How can I force him to accept an award he seems not to want?"

The major pulled the doctor towards an area of more privacy as he made his case. "Listen, since we beat the Spaniards, we now have land possessions around the world. Almost overnight, we've become an imperial nation. This means we'll be more involved in what's going on all around the world. In order to do that, we'll need soldiers and sailors. It's a miracle we won with the number of troops that we currently have, but we're going to need far more to be ready for the next one. In order to get troops—we need heroes. We need to inspire people to join up. Sergeant Hayes's story is just what we need. So, if he accepts the award—we get to tell his story."

The doctor glanced back towards Cuz before asking the major, "How much time do I have to convince him?"

"Time is not our friend. Four months ago a bunch of Chinese started killing Christians in hopes of starting some type of campaign to run all of the foreigners out of their country. We may have to go protect American citizens living there in just a few months. There are a lot of people in China and right now, our numbers are really low."

The doctor slowly nodded. "I'll work as fast as I can to make sure he accepts the award."

It took two full days for Cuz to stabilize from his tirade in front of the major. The doctor planned to speak with him for the first time since the incident when he completed his morning rounds. Just before seeing Cuz, Captain Hodge stopped briefly to check on his patient from the bayou.

"Well, doc, you was right. This here paper says it snowed all over the place!"

"Even in New Orleans?"

"Yes, doc. Even in New Orleans. Paper says they's gonna call the storm, 'The Snow King' cause they never seen such a thang. Why's they have to name the storm any-way? Why not just call it the 'Mardi Gras of 1899' storm?"

"Well, I guess one name is as good as another. Hey, you could call it the Valentine's Day Snow."

The patient sat up and in a quieter voice asked the doctor, "Hey, doc, which nurse is Darthula? Is she the tall one or the one with red hair?"

The doctor meditated on the question for a second and replied, "Not sure who Darthula is. Why do you ask?"

"On account of I got this here note from her say'n how she hopes I get to feel'n better so as maybe I can takes her dance'n when I heal up better. You sure it's not the tall one or maybe the red-haired one?"

With confidence, Captain Hodge replied, "I'm certain your admirer is neither of the women you think. The tall nurse is Nurse Sherry and the other is Nurse Jessica." After making a notation in the patient's chart, the doctor had a thought. "Hey, you know, Darthula may be Nurse D from the north wing. She sometimes works over here in the early morning hours to help out."

"Is she good look'n?"

"Since I'm a married man, I don't notice such things." The doctor turned to leave but paused long enough to remark, "However, I can tell you that if Darthula is Nurse D, she's missing two front teeth and has a lazy eye. But, she's from Louisiana, like you, so you two could trade stories about gumbo and frog-gigging."

The patient asked Nurse Jessica who had just arrived, "He's pull'n my leg about her looks, right?"

Jessica maintained a blank expression as she replied, "Yes, he's joking." Then, just as the patient started to relax slightly, she added, "She's missing four teeth."

Walking towards Cuz, the doctor saw him squirm slightly in his bed. As the doctor neared the bed, Cuz raised one hand and started to address his reaction from a couple of days earlier. The doctor interrupted him and asked, "How are your burns faring?" When Cuz tried again to speak of his protest, the doctor read aloud from the chart. "Looks like your fever has gone for now. There's some noticeable strength returning to your legs."

"Aren't you going to try talking me into accepting that award?"

Captain Hodge kept his eyes focused on the patient's chart as he made some notes. After a brief delay, he answered Cuz's question. "What's there to discuss? You acted in an unselfish manner under enemy fire and saved not just one or two, but 15 fellow soldiers. Your commanding officer wants to acknowledge your heroism by awarding you the Medal of Honor. Now, for some reason, you believe you want to refuse the recognition. Does that about sum it up?"

Cuz's face became defiant as he clenched his fists. "I ain't no hero, and I don't want no award!"

Setting the chart down, the doctor took a conciliatory approach. "Sometimes it's not about what you want but rather what those 15 soldiers want. It's about the Army not wanting to be accused of ignoring such a courageous effort. It's about your commanding officer's leadership abilities of inspiring the other men under his command by emphasizing those efforts they deem truly noteworthy." Pausing only briefly for the previous points to sink in, he continued, "Frankly, I don't understand why you wouldn't want to receive the medal—you earned it!"

Cuz and the doctor debated the issue for nearly 10 minutes before Cuz grew weary. "Listen, doc, I don't deserve it. You see, I've done things in the past—bad things. I had to run away from home because of it. I don't know how else to say it—I'm just not worthy!"

"Sergeant, the Army doesn't care about some youthful indiscretion. For that matter, recognizing your efforts in battle doesn't depend upon on any of your accomplishments or deficiencies before your military service."

Cuz lifted himself slightly from his bed as he exclaimed, "What about murder?"

"Whom did you murder?"

Cuz started to respond, but then realized he had already said too much. "Doc, I've already said my piece. I don't deserve no award. Now, I'm sorry, sir, but I'm really tired and feel a bit sickly. Maybe we can continue this talk some other time?"

Captain Hodge realized that Cuz was adamant about not accepting the Medal of Honor. Of more of a concern for him as a doctor was Cuz's firm belief that he had murdered someone. Was this a new psychological development stemming from his malaria-fueled delusions, or did he actually murder someone before joining the Army?

Heading to his office, Captain Hodge was already planning his strategy for his next discussion with Cuz. Suddenly, Nurse Sherry broke into his concentration. "Excuse me, doctor, Colonel Dean requests you see him in his office right away."

"Thank you, nurse." The captain immediately proceeded to his commanding officer's office.

Wondering why he was being summoned, he initially thought he would be assigned to join Major Walter Reed on his Typhoid Fever Board. Certainly such activities would benefit his career as well as possibly allow him to work on research into malaria and yellow fever. However, the captain wondered if he would have enough time to continue working with his patients.

Shortly after he arrived at Colonel Dean's office, the captain learned the purpose of the meeting. "I understand you have a patient who is being awarded the Medal of Honor."

"Yes, sir. Sergeant Hayes."

"What's this nonsense about him refusing the award?"

"Yes, sir. The sergeant has stated that he doesn't want..."

"Who does he think he is? He can't refuse the Medal of Honor! What if his actions had killed him? He couldn't refuse it then. Isn't that correct?"

The captain started to respond, but Colonel Dean continued, "I understand this man is from Memphis. Didn't they teach him manners down there? Doesn't he know it isn't polite to turn down such an honor?"

The captain muttered, "Polite, sir?"

"Yes, you heard me! It's not polite to turn down something that you are being given!"

"Excuse me, sir, but I don't believe that's the way Sergeant Hayes sees it."

"Listen here, captain! The Army is giving him the Medal of Honor, and he's going to accept it! Is that understood?"

"It's not that simple, sir. He sincerely believes he doesn't deserve it."

"Cripes! There are 15 soldiers who believe he is deserving, not to mention his commanding officer and the commander of the Sixth Cavalry. It's not his place to say that he's not deserving!"

"Yes, sir. I understand that. However, Sergeant Hayes believes he's undeserving of the medal since he believes he murdered someone before entering military service."

"He believes he murdered someone? What kind of rubbish is that? Either he did, or he didn't. What's all this about believing that he did?"

"Sergeant Hayes, in addition to his battle wounds, is also suffering from malaria. He has had several fits as the result of prolonged high fever. These fits have given him several delusions. At this time, we are not sure if this alleged murder is fact or just another one of his vivid delusions."

Colonel Dean considered carefully what he had just heard. He then asked a couple of medical-related questions regarding Cuz's overall health. Pausing briefly to stare out of his window, the colonel turned quickly and asked, "Captain, isn't your wife from Tennessee?"

"Yes, sir. Her mother lives in Memphis."

"Excellent! You can take her home for a couple of weeks. While there, you're going to find out what you can to convince Sergeant Hayes that he didn't murder anyone. Maybe after you convince him that this is nothing more than his mind playing tricks on him, he'll come around and accept the Medal of Honor. Then, we can all put this unfortunate business behind us."

"Sir, what happens if I find out that he really did murder someone?"

The colonel stood up straight and confidently stated, "Captain, you're a fine doctor. You are being sent to Memphis to research this matter. I believe wearing the hats of an Army captain, an Army doctor, and a researcher gives you enough to do for now. Don't take on the role of judge and jury just yet. If you find out there's been a murder, we'll cross that bridge when we get to it."

After some final instructions, the captain returned to his office. Once he had updated all of his patient's files so they could be temporarily turned over to a replacement he met with Nurse Sherry and Nurse Jessica. The three of them compared notes on what they knew about Cuz and his life in Memphis.

Once his preparations were complete, the captain went home to inform his wife of their sudden trip to visit her mother. Naturally, Polly was excited about going back home for a visit, but was skeptical as to the true reason. Fortunately, the captain would have ample time to explain the full story to her on their journey there.

Chapter Two

The Arrival

After a lengthy and arduous journey, the captain and his wife finally arrived in Memphis. While Polly was excited to see her mother for the first time in several months, the captain was a little apprehensive.

On the carriage ride from the station, he muttered, "I never know what to call your mother."

"Don't be silly! Just call her mother like I do."

"I can't do that. She's not my mother. The last time I was here, she wanted me to call her Lavinia. I can't do that either since it seems so disrespectful."

Polly laughed. "You're spending far too much time worrying about something so meaningless."

The captain just turned to watch the passing city images as they made their way to their destination. The city had cleaned itself up noticeably since the last time he had visited.

Once the carriage stopped at the end of Eastmoreland Avenue, Polly's mother came running from the house to greet her guests. After a lengthy hug with her daughter and a polite hug for her son-in-law, the captain said, "Hello, Mrs. Reiley. We're very happy to be here."

Polly smirked at her husband's speaking to her mother so formally.

Mrs. Reiley just tilted her head slightly and replied, "Now, Daniel, we talked about this the last time you were here. Please call me Lavinia. Now both of you come inside—there's so much for us to talk about."

The captain and Polly avoided telling her mother about the real reason for their trip to Memphis out of fear that she would be hurt to learn the visit wasn't just to see her. The captain said, "Some work associates requested me to deliver some messages on their behalf."

Lavinia replied, "Messages? What kind of messages?"

Before the captain could reply, Polly stated, "Mother! If you entrusted a personal message to someone to deliver for you, would you want them telling everyone about it? These messages could be very personal in nature. I'm sure Daniel's associates wouldn't appreciate him violating their confidences. Wouldn't you agree?"

With a suspicious look, Lavinia nodded and said, "Would either of you like some more cake?"

After breakfast the following morning, the captain left the house to begin his investigation. He thought he'd go first to the police station to find out about any murders that may have occurred around the time Gunsie Hayes ran away from Memphis.

The station was very busy for a Monday. Trying to find someone who could assist him proved challenging. Eventually, he was introduced to Sergeant Allen Vickery. The sergeant was in charge of records and was intrigued by the captain's interest in a possible unsolved murder around August 1882.

Sergeant Vickery said, "I'm not often asked about 17-year-old murders. Mostly just the occasional church-goer wanting to know if a solicitation or public drunkenness charge was really purged from the records like their lawyer told them. Who was supposed to have been murdered and why are you interested in it?"

Wanting to disguise his true intent, the captain replied, "Well, you see, sergeant, there's this hole in our records, and the Army sent me here to see if I could find some answers. All we know was that this man may have been murdered in August of 1882."

The sergeant retrieved a book from a shelf as he replied, "So this murdered guy was an Army guy, but you don't know his name? That's kind of strange, ain't it? How do you know he was murdered if you don't even know his name?"

Not wanting to spin a stickier web of deception than he had already managed in such a short time, the captain answered, "The Army loses records all the time. I'm just trying to fill in some blanks."

Sergeant Vickery let out a faint groan as if he wasn't totally convinced by the captain's reasoning. Nonetheless, he continued scanning the records for the timeframe provided. Turning the page, he asked, "Was this Army hero fellow killed by vigilantes?"

The captain thought about the question for a moment before replying, "No, I don't think so."

Meanwhile, he started to consider the possibility that Cuz murdered someone while part of some vigilante group. If that were the case, why would Cuz have felt the need to shoulder the guilt all by himself? Certainly if this had been the case, he would have said, "We killed Stumpy,' rather than taking the sole responsibility.

After several minutes of searching over the records and murmuring various offenses, "...drunk, drunk and disorderly, bar fight, peeping, bar fight, drunk, hey, here's a bar fight where a guy was stabbed. Oh, never mind, it looks like the victim lived...", the sergeant shut the book and announced, "Well, captain, I reviewed all of our records from July to September of 1882, and there are no unsolved murders."

Slowly nodding, the captain smiled and said, "Well, at least we know he wasn't murdered."

"It may be more complicated than that. These records only show situations where charges were filed or allegations were actually made official. There are many lynchings and suspicious deaths that wouldn't show up here."

The captain looked perplexed. The sergeant then said, "You may want to check with the newspaper. They may have the most complete listing of deaths in the area."

Looking as if he'd thought of something important, the sergeant then added, "If you go there, make sure you ask for Ellisson Nuttal."

Pleased that at least he had another lead, the captain sought clarification. "So this Mr. Nuttal works for the *Appeal-Avalanche*?"

The sergeant chuckled slightly as he replied, "You've been away for a while, haven't you? *The Appeal-Avalanche* got bought up by *The Memphis Commercial* about five or six years ago. They now call themselves *The Commercial Appeal* and they are located at 40 Madison. But, no, the newspaper where you can find Mr. Nuttal is *The Scimitar*. They are located closer to the river at 13 Madison, I believe. I think Mr. Nuttal is retired, but he still keeps an office there just to keep up appearances."

Before the captain left, the sergeant offered, "I got some pork sandwiches and cornbread my momma made for me if you want some. There's plenty here."

Although the food looked delicious, the captain declined so he could hurry over to *The Scimitar.*

Walking into the newspaper offices, the captain was promptly greeted by an older gentleman who slowly rose from a desk in the main room. As soon as the captain stated that he was looking for Mr. Ellisson Nuttal, the tall lanky man quickly replied, "Are you from the courthouse or the sheriff's department?"

The captain stammered, "Neither. I'm a captain in the United States Army doing research about a man who was supposedly murdered in Memphis back in August of 1882. I was told that you may be able to help me research this matter."

"Well, then, won't you please step into my office so that we can discuss this research of yours in more detail?"

As the two men got situated in the small cluttered office, the captain said, "Mr. Nuttal, my name is Captain Daniel Hodge. I'm an army doctor..."

He was interrupted as Mr. Nuttal raised his hand and interjected, "Please, call me Eli. Now, you say your name is Daniel Hodge?"

The captain nodded and began to continue to tell him what he was investigating when Eli tilted his head slightly and asked, "You any relation to a Daniel Hodge who rode with the Fourth Regiment Georgia Volunteer Cavalry?"

"Yes, sir, he was my father. He served under Captain Hughes Houston Burke."

Eli sprang to his feet and reached across the desk to shake the captain's hand. Surprised, the captain quickly rose to his feet as well and reached to shake Eli's hand.

Eli quickly explained, "Your father saved my father's life in action outside of Dalton, Georgia. They were both in the same regiment when my father's horse got shot out from under him. The Yanks were coming in fast, and your father doubled back and snatched him up just in time. At least, that's the way my father told the story. For that, I want to thank you for what your father did. Is he still alive?"

Smiling with pride hearing this story of his father's heroism for the first time, he somberly responded, "No, sir. He died back in 1886. He didn't talk much about the war. Whenever he was asked about it, he would just respond, 'We lost.'"

Gesturing for the captain to return to his seat, Eli said, "Well, I am honored to meet you. Now, what can I do for you?"

Processing the exchange he just had encouraged him to reevaluate his approach. Rather than being secretive and vague about his quest, the captain decided to level with Eli and rely upon the respect he had for the senior Daniel Hodge to keep the inquiry confidential.

After sharing everything he knew about Gunsie Hayes and the alleged murder of some guy named Stumpy, the captain watched as Eli digested the information with the curiosity of a seasoned reporter.

Eli then leaned forward and described what he thought should be the next steps in "their" investigation. "I will research our old newspaper archives for any mention of

Hayes or 'Stumpy' and see what I can find. I'll also look for any suspicious deaths in the summer of '82."

While Eli was telling the captain what he was going to research, he was carefully printing some information on a piece of paper. As he finished, he laughed softly and clarified, "Of course, when I said I would research, I meant to say that J.B. would be doing the research."

Eli stepped out of his office and called loudly for J.B. Returning to the front of his desk, Eli explained that J.B. was his research savant. "I can give J.B. these names and words, and she will quickly read every newspaper in our collection. If they are in our archives, she'll find them."

The captain sensed someone at the office door so he rose from his chair and turned to greet J.B. However, Eli motioned for the captain to not approach her and to speak very softly to her.

He said, "Hello, my name is Captain Hodge. Are you J.B?"

She didn't respond, continuing to look down at the floor. Eli took a step closer to her as he offered her the paper. "Can you please see if you can find these words in the old editions?"

With both hands, she took the paper and looked at it carefully. After a moment, she nodded and then quickly walked away.

"Does she ever speak?"

Eli replied, "Only occasionally. Her name is Johanna Bales. I know her father—he advertises in our paper. He invited me over once for dinner. That's when he ambushed me with the notion that I could get her a job here at the paper. I was reluctant at first but she has turned out to be a great asset when it comes to researching. She's also a fantastic violin player. Listen to this, she can play from memory songs she's seen written somewhere before or heard played previously by someone else."

"That's remarkable!"

"Yes. Why don't you return tomorrow to see if J.B. has found anything regarding our case?"

When he got home, Polly and her mother met him as he walked in the front door. Polly gave him a big kiss and asked how his day had been. Polly's mother smiled and emphasized her greeting, "Hello, Daniel."

Puzzled, he just returned the smile and offered a friendly "Hello."

Polly and her mother exchanged glances as they slightly chuckled.

As Lavinia went into the kitchen leaving Polly and her husband alone, he quietly asked her, "What was that all about?"

"She's just waiting for you to call her Lavinia."

He just smirked before telling her how the investigation was going. She shared his excitement as he told her about learning that his father had saved Eli's father during the war. He then told her about J.B. and her unusual talents.

While they were discussing his day, he noticed that his mouth was beginning to water and his stomach begin to growl. "Something smells good in the kitchen! What's for dinner?"

Polly replied, "It's chicken and dumplings night."

The captain smiled.

After dinner, the three sat in the front room while they sipped their potent homemade elderberry wine. George Reiley, Lavinia's current husband, made wine whenever he wasn't working as a civil engineer for railroad expansion in the outlands, specifically Texas. He wasn't around much, but he wired most of his paycheck home each Wednesday.

After a slight cough to clear his throat, the captain blurted, "I swear I've had Georgia hooch that didn't pack this much of a punch!"

Polly and Lavinia smiled and nodded as they continued to sip their drinks.

The captain brought the wine bottle closer as he studied the homemade label. "Does Mr. Reiley make much of this stuff?"

Lavinia dabbed the perspiration from her cheeks and forehead before responding. "He makes a few bottles whenever he's home. Every now and then, I give a bottle to some ladies at the U.D.C. meetings. I also donate a bottle or two to the Nineteenth Century Club for charity auctions. I hear they are quite popular and usually fetch a nice donation for their cause."

The three sat in silence for a time while they each appreciated George's wine.

Late the next morning, the captain arrived back at Eli's office. Looking around the large outer office for Eli, he noticed him near the back wall speaking to J.B. He waved to her as she turned and apparently left out a back door. Once he noticed the captain, he rapidly moved towards him, exclaiming, "I think we've found some useful information to help us get started!"

As the two got settled in Eli's office, he began to relay their findings. "J.B.'s been researching since you left here yesterday. I even took her over to the other paper's archives as we looked over what they had."

He shuffled his notes around so that he could present the findings to the captain. "The only time we found anything on Gunsie Hayes was in an article back in 1868 talking about the death of a lady by the name of Austina Hayes who was married to a man named Christopher. The article said that she was survived by a three-year-old son named Gunsie."

The captain thought about this just long enough to do some basic calculations. "That sounds about right since he's 34 now."

Eli turned over a page of his notes and then continued. "There was an obituary a few days later that stated Austina was the daughter of Mr. and Mrs. Paul Metzger." Eli looked at the captain and said, "If this is the same Paul Metzger that I'm thinking of, he owned a bakery over on Linden near Orleans."

The captain started making some notes of his own as Eli continued. "J.B. then found several articles on Austina's death. The earlier articles said that she had been attacked while later articles reported that it was just a tragic accident."

The captain sat forward as he asked, "So, we're saying Gunsie's mother died under suspicious circumstances and 14 years later Gunsie supposedly murdered somebody?"

Eli nodded as he said, "Listen to this. I may have found out who 'Stumpy' was. Once we started looking for anything on Christopher Hayes, we found three or four articles. The earliest one we found was talking about a delivery company that was expanding and all of the great things they were doing for their customers, and the like. Anyway, it mentioned a couple of their prominent draymen, one of whom was Christopher Hayes. The article went on to say that he was one of their fastest draymen despite having lost his left arm in the war."

"So you think Stumpy is Gunsie's father? Are we saying that we think Gunsie thinks he murdered his own father?"

Eli hesitantly nodded. "We couldn't find anything about Christopher Hayes' death. We also looked around August of 1882 and didn't see anything about anyone by the name of Hayes dying. J.B. did find a record of a guy by the name of Luke Hayes who died of yellow fever in 1878. After that, the trail disappears."

The captain pondered aloud. "So, Gunsie holds his father responsible in some way for his mother's death and when he gets older he murders the man he believes is guilty—maybe, but if Christopher was murdered in 1882, where is his body? Luke Hayes, who is he? How does he figure into all of this? Is he a relative? Maybe he had family who knew more details about Christopher and Gunsie."

Eli looked back at his notes and said, "Well, Luke died at the temporary hospital that was set up over at St. Agnes Academy. Maybe one of the nuns remembers him or has some records that could help."

"Temporary hospital?"

Eli leaned back in his chair and replied, "Back in the spring of 1878, St. Agnes Academy burned to the ground. Over the next few months, they quickly rebuilt and right when they were announcing that they'd be open for the fall term, the city was stricken with the worst yellow fever epidemic of all. While the previous epidemics claimed the lives of a few hundred, the epidemic of 1873 claimed almost 2,000 deaths. So, it's little wonder that when the fever returned in 1878, there was widespread panic. Everyone left the city. Neighbors, friends, police, doctors, nurses...they all ran away. The only ones left were folks too sick or too poor to leave. The nuns over at St. Agnes stayed. They converted their new building into a makeshift hospital and attempted to care for everyone who couldn't get treated by the meager contingent of doctors and nurses who stayed behind at the regular hospital. The remaining Protestants did something similar thanks largely to some members of the Episcopal sisterhood from Peekskill, New York. They turned St. Mary's School into a temporary hospital as well."

"Was it as bad as everyone feared?"

"No, it was worse! Over 5,100 died. On average, there were 200 deaths each day. Corpses were everywhere. Of the 41 police officers in the city, only seven survived. One by one, they died at their posts."

The two men sat in silence. Eli broke it by interjecting, "They say it was the most yellow fever deaths in an inland city ever, but it didn't keep our city from holding its annual carnival. I guess the survivors appreciated the gorgeous pageants just a bit more that year."

Agreeing to follow up on the lead regarding Luke Hayes, the captain headed for the door. Before leaving, he turned and asked, "St. Agnes is the one over at Third and Polar, isn't it?"

Eli corrected him. "That used to be called the St. Agnes Academy Day School but is now called the Notre Dame De La Sallette. You need to go to the St Agnes Academy over on Vance between Orleans and Brinkley."

"Thanks. Please pass along my appreciation to J.B. as well."

Once he arrived at St. Agnes Academy, he went directly to the office where he encountered Sister Basil. She immediately presented herself as an extremely stern force not prone to small talk. Therefore, the captain jumped quickly to his request. "I understand that a gentleman by the name of Luke Hayes died here of yellow fever back in the fall of 1878."

With her arms folded in front of her, Sister Basil unsympathetically looked at the captain without response.

Flashing back to dealings with his drill sergeant in boot camp several years earlier, the captain continued, "I just need to confirm his death and to determine if your records show his next of kin."

"Are you Catholic?" she asked.

After a slight stammer, the captain answered, "No, does that matter?"

Glaring as if angered the captain dared to answer a question with a question, she asked, "Was Mr. Hayes Catholic?"

As the captain again started to ask, "Is it important?" Sister Basil firmly interjected, "Catholics' records are separate from non-Catholics' records. How am I to determine which set of records to search?"

"Can't you check both?"

Sister Basil's anger grew with yet another question in response to her question. In a huff, she turned and walked around a partition and out of sight. Taking note of a beautiful piece of blue quartz on the counter, he reached to pick it up when suddenly he heard Sister Basil command, "Don't touch the quartz!"

He immediately thought, "How did she know I was reaching for the quartz?" Looking around the room he saw no windows or mirrors that could have helped her see his actions. As he leaned to peer around the partition, he heard a file drawer shut as she quickly returned to the desk.

"Yes, Luke Hayes died here on October 4, 1878, and the only known relatives listed were two sons: Cuz Hayes and Ira Gleason."

Shocked, he blurted, "How can that be? Cuz's parents were Christopher and Austina. Who is Luke?"

Sister Basil snipped back, "During the yellow plague, 15 Catholic priests and 30 sisters died in their heroic battle to tend to the sick. Our files are filled with the names of thousands who suffered and died on these grounds. Certainly, you do not believe I would know why Luke is listed as these boys' father as opposed to Christopher."

Considering his words carefully, he asked, "Sister, please tell me, isn't there anyone still around who may have known these people? I wouldn't ask if it wasn't important."

After taking a deep breath, Sister Basil suggested, "Sister Margarete will be back here tomorrow. She was with St. Agnes Academy in 1878. You can come back and speak to her."

The captain thanked Sister Basil for her assistance as he glanced once again at the blue quartz. He started to ask her how she knew he was about to touch the quartz earlier. However, once he looked at her to ask his question, her stone-faced expression changed only slightly as her right eyebrow raised into a pointed arch. He decided he didn't need to know and just smiled at her before he left.

Stopping by *The Scimitar* briefly, the captain updated Eli on his findings. The two agreed that they needed to search the records for anything linking Christopher and Luke Hayes. They also needed to see what they could learn about this alleged brother of Gunsie. Who was Ira Gleason and why did he have a different last name?

Eli promised to get J.B. on it as soon as she came back to work. "After working all night last night, I may not see her again until tomorrow. No matter, one of us will start searching for information first thing in the morning."

With the day's work wrapped up, the captain headed back home. All the way there, he was summoning the strength to call his mother-in-law Lavinia. Upon opening the door, he found Polly and her mother standing there awaiting his arrival.

As soon as Polly gave her husband a welcome-home kiss, Lavinia said, "Hello, Daniel. Did you have a nice day?"

Regardless of his lengthy preparation and courage he thought he had harnessed, he replied, "Hello, Mrs. Reiley. I had a very interesting day. What did the two of you do today?"

Polly rolled her eyes and slowly shook her head as Lavinia sighed and walked back to the kitchen.

Chapter Three

Sister Margarete

Mid-morning on Wednesday, the captain went back to St. Agnes Academy to meet Sister Margarete. It was a sunny morning with a spring-like breeze in the air, different from what they had recently been suffering from.

Reaching for the front door of the academy offices, the captain heard his name called from behind him. Turning to identify the source, he spotted a nun who appeared to be 40 or 50. She had plump rosy cheeks and beautiful eyes that had a slight glint of mischief in them.

After confirming that she was Sister Margarete, he had to ask, "How did you know I was Captain Hodge?"

While smiling and pointing to his uniform, she replied, "How many army captains do you think visit us here at St. Agnes Academy?"

Immediately, the captain found himself much more at ease speaking with Sister Margarete than he had been with Sister Basil. He said, "Please forgive me if I appeared a bit startled. I guess I thought you were Sister Basil."

Sister Margarete instantly donned a serious face and lowered her voice an octave or two as she blurted, "Are you Catholic?"

The captain became totally confused but before he could reply, Sister Margarete laughed. "I'm just giving you my best impression of Sister Basil!"

Again, the captain felt much more at ease and explained to Sister Margarete the purpose of his visit. Specifically, he was trying to learn as much as possible about Gunsie Hayes and his father. "By any chance did you know either of them?"

With a nod and a smile, she acknowledged that she knew the Hayes family. As she collected her thoughts, she began to slowly walk across the yard. She began, "Austina Metzger was Gunsie's mother."

The captain provided a knowing nod before she continued. "The Metzgers had the best bakery. I went there as often as I could afford. Their strudels were scrumptious. At Christmas time, they had the most wonderful cookies: lebkuchen, pfeffernusse, and springerle. They made this iced molasses that was just divine." She paused momentarily as she fondly reflected on the enjoyable treats. "Sometimes when I had no money, I would go in there just to smell their creations. Austina knew when I couldn't buy anything so she would slip me a sweet German pretzel as she winked at me. She was a wonderful lady."

Thinking he would treat her to some of her favorite pastries in appreciation for her answering his questions, he asked, "Is the bakery still there?"

In a reflective tone, she responded, "No, all the Metzgers and the bakery are all gone now. There's an Italian bakery called Spada's over on Union, but their cannoli are a little too dry for my liking. However, Sister Basil seems to enjoy them."

After a brief laugh, he encouraged her to continue.

"It was magical from the first day Austina met Christopher. He was a one-armed drayman who always seemed to be delivering something to the bakery. Austina seemed to insist on him moving the delivery from spot to spot inside the storeroom just to delay his departure. Then, they would start discussing fruit pies in a manner... Well, I'll just say that it would make you blush. By the time he left the store, all the customers who had witnessed the discussion were lined up to buy whatever fruit pie was available. It was a sight, I tell you!"

"How did Christopher lose his arm?"

"I believe that happened at Shiloh. They say he was helping a wounded Yank when two other Yanks shot him. He never let it keep him from doing anything! I saw him switch from a two-horse to a four-horse team faster than any man I know who has the full use of both arms."

Sister Margarete reflected briefly before continuing. "The two of them were wonderful together. When they had Gunsie, it was certainly the picture of a perfect family. Tragedy struck when Austina died in November of 1868. They said it was an accident."

Interrupting, the captain observed, "You sound as if there's some doubt that it was an accident."

"It's not my place to judge," she quickly replied. "I'm certain you can find plenty of others who would gladly render an opinion on the matter since there were many unanswered questions. In any event, the fact remained that she died when Gunsie was only three. Christopher tried to do his best taking care of the young boy, but between his work and the cost of a full-time nanny, he just couldn't do it. After wrestling with his conscience for several weeks, he reluctantly placed Gunsie in St. Peter's Orphanage the following January."

Looking up from his note taking, the captain asked, "What about the Metzgers? Couldn't they have taken care of Gunsie?"

After taking a deep breath, she continued, "Austina's mother died of yellow fever in the summer of '67. The stress weighed terribly on Mr. Metzger. Austina helped him as much as she could, but especially when she died, his depression was just too much for him to bear. He went into the asylum about five weeks after Austina's death—it was on Christmas Day, as I remember."

The captain asked, "Gunsie was very young at the time. Did he grow to become angry with his father for leaving him at an orphanage?"

Flashing a look of surprise, she replied, "Angry at Christopher? He may have been sad at times, but Gunsie grew to realize how fortunate he was. Christopher went to the orphanage two or three times every month and would take Gunsie home for the weekend. If Christopher had a delivery near St. Peters, he would always stop in to have lunch with his son. Then, once Gunsie was around nine, Christopher removed both him and his friend from the orphanage permanently."

The captain interjected, "This friend of Gunsie's, was that the Ira who was listed as Christopher's son on the St. Agnes records?"

"Yes, Christopher adopted Ira and treated him like close family. Ira was around 12 when he moved in with them."

Again, the captain interjected, "The three of them lived as a family until Christopher died in October of 1878, is that correct?"

"Yes, that's correct. The boys went to school and did well, as I understand it. Ira looked after Gunsie until Christopher got home from work. One afternoon, when I stopped by to say hello, the two boys were prodding each other to hurry up and finish their home studies so that they could go fishing. Evidently, they had found a good spot to catch panfish."

The captain looked up quickly and asked, "Did they tell you where this fishing spot was?"

Sister Margarete just laughed and said, "If they did mention the location, I would've forgotten it by now." Then, with a sigh, she confirmed that Christopher died of yellow fever in the autumn of '78.

When asked if she was with Christopher when he died, Sister Margarete appeared to become slightly defensive. "No, I wasn't here at the time. I was assigned duties elsewhere. I didn't learn of his death until after I returned in November of that year."

Both kept quiet for a moment. Sister Margarete took a deep breath and said, "Most people just don't understand what it was like once the yellow plague struck. Back in 1873, they say the city lost nearly 2,000 people to the fever. I saw the dedication of the sisters here and the clergy throughout the city to care for the ill and comfort the survivors. That was when I received my calling. By the time I took my vows and joined the sisters here at St. Agnes, it wasn't long before the fever returned in 1878."

She stopped for a second to breathe in the fresh spring breeze before continuing, "In July we heard the fever had struck New Orleans and Vicksburg. The city began to panic as they blocked riverboats from discharging any passengers from there or any other areas that the plague was known to be. They set up a large quarantine camp on President's Island and made people who were from infected areas wear yellow jackets. Then, for a couple of weeks, the citizens waited to see if the containment would work."

The captain was spellbound listening to her firsthand account of how yellow fever attacked the city. She continued, "In August, a restaurant owner got the fever and died. After that, it spread quickly throughout Memphis. Yellow flags were displayed along the river banks warning riverboat passengers of the fever's presence."

"Within one week, over 25,000 people picked up and left. Can you imagine? Twenty-five thousand friends and neighbors left within a single week. Many ran off so quickly that they left their front doors open and abandoned much of their possessions. Doctors, bankers, preachers, nurses, contractors, city workers, morticians...no matter what walk of life, they all picked up and left in panic. The only folks who seemed to have stayed behind were those who were too poor or frail to leave."

"Certainly not everyone left?"

"No, several stayed here out of their dedication to serve. Some people even traveled here from other cities just to help care for the sick. Many who tried to leave were stopped at blockades around the city. The surrounding communities didn't want yellow fever to spread to their towns so they stopped many of the fleeing masses and sent them back to Memphis. Of the residents who stayed behind, 17,000 got the fever and over 5,000 died from it."

Walking around the corner of a hedgerow, the captain and Sister Margarete came upon two girls who were apparently trying to skip a class. Sister Margarete challenged, "Ladies! Don't you have someplace you need to be?"

The two young students were scared speechless at being discovered and quickly scurried back to class.

"They need constant supervision," she explained before continuing with her description of the events surrounding the 1878 yellow fever epidemic in Memphis. "Everyone knew that the chance of survival was low if we stayed. I was prepared and ready to stay. I was needed here. However, the Mother Superior had other ideas. The number of orphans was growing daily. They too would certainly die if they stayed in the city."

The captain looked confused since he couldn't understand where else the children could go. After all, the city was effectively barricaded on all sides preventing transit to safer areas.

Sister Margarete nodded slowly as she continued, "The Mother Superior's plan was to send the orphans to one of the refugee camps that had sprung up in areas away from Memphis. I was told that I would be the one to escort the orphans through the blockades. I immediately requested that she reconsider my selection for the assignment since I believed I would be far more useful remaining behind. Suzanne responded before the Mother Superior could accept that I had dared challenge her decision..."

"Suzanne?" the captain inquired.

Smiling and then blushing slightly, Sister Margarete explained. "Several of the ladies who worked in brothels around town stepped up and took on nursing duties and cared for the sick as needed. One Memphis Madam, Miss Annie Cook, turned her brothel into a temporary hospital After she died of the fever, she became known as 'Mary Magdalene of Memphis.' Some of the other ladies decided to come and assist us here at St. Agnes. Suzanne Dugan was one of these ladies. Anyway, she heard my request to send someone else to escort the orphans out of town and she just blurted back, 'They'd never let a painted lady through the barrier no matter how many young'uns she had with her! A nun escort is their only hope!'"

The captain could see a small tear roll down her cheek as she recalled the story. She quickly brushed the tear away as she continued. "Mother Superior agreed, and there was nothing more that could be said. So, I left that afternoon with 17 boys and girls who were all recently orphaned because of the yellow plague. We marched right through the barricades for White's Station and for Neshoba without any problem. We settled in a camp near Forest Hill and stayed there until the first of November."

Her eyes grew watery as she described her return to St. Agnes. "Thirty nuns bravely stood their ground here and died while they tended to the suffering of others. Sixteen priests also died of the fever. There were plenty of others besides Catholics who died because of the plague; St. Mary's Episcopal Church also lost several of their nuns and priests to the disease as well."

Again, the two of them stood quietly for a moment as she composed herself to continue. "That's when I learned Christopher had died and that Suzanne had taken the boys to live with her."

The captain was shocked. "What did you say? Why would this Suzanne take in two boys to live with her... in a brothel?"

After briefly thinking about the question, she gasped as she apologized to the captain. "Oh, I understand your confusion. You are unaware that Suzanne and Austina were childhood friends from when they both lived up in Raleigh. As I understand it, when Suzanne was only five, her father left to go fight in the Mexican War and was never seen or heard from again. In the early 1850s, Austina and her family moved down here to start their bakery. Suzanne kept in touch through letters. Once typhoid killed Suzanne's mother and paternal grandparents, she bounced around from distant relatives to family friends. Eventually, an aunt here in Memphis was persuaded to allow her to come stay with her family."

"Once those two girls reconnected down here in Memphis, they were inseparable. About a year later, another girl joined these two, and the three were great friends—almost like close sisters. This new girl was Winnie Clay. I never knew much about Winnie other than to recognize how rapidly she developed an interest in men."

Sister Margarete stopped her story to ask the captain for the correct time. As he pulled out his pocket watch, she smiled and suggested that they sit on a bench nearby for a while. Evidently, she was lying in wait for some more class skippers.

She then continued, "As the three young ladies grew up, their attention turned to more adult interests and goals. Austina was determined to be of assistance to her father in the family bakery business. Suzanne met a young lad in school and quickly married. She worked as a dress-maker for a few dollars a week. She had dreams of owning her own store someday if she could save enough money. Meanwhile, Winnie was very mature for her age and courted several young men. Her parents encouraged this behavior in hopes that she too would get married and move out onto her own. In short, they were anxious to reduce the burden of feeding and caring for her."

"When the War Between the States broke out, Austina and her parents continued to operate the bakery and tried to maintain their lives as much as they could to what they had before the war."

"Suzanne's husband was an abusive man who drank heavily and with increasing regularity throughout their stormy two years of marriage. When Tennessee seceded in 1861, he shouted about killing Yankees during one of his drunken rages at the local bar. When a group of Southern sympathizers approached him to join the Confederate military, he started to back down from his loud rhetoric. This led to accusations of cowardice, which enraged him. He either had to face being a coward or enlist to prove his loyalty. Demanding a moment to gather his wits and ponder the situation more carefully, he stepped out into the street. As many of the bar patrons looked on, he took off running. That was the last time anyone saw him. Everyone thought he ran off to the outlands. No matter where he went, Suzanne had been abandoned to fend for herself."

The captain asked, "The outlands? Do you mean Arkansas or Texas?"

"As lazy as he was, I'd be surprised if he made it past Arkansas."

She continued with her story. "Winnie's father and oldest brother left to join the Rebels while her youngest brother left to join the Federals. In December of 1861, her mother died of consumption. Winnie was now all alone, but her skill of manipulating men served her well as she moved into a boardinghouse full of prostitutes. While her income was more than any of her friends, after the Yanks occupied the city in June of 1862, her income grew to more than most of the citizenry."

With a disappointed sigh, Sister Margarete continued, "Suzanne quickly saw the potential of Winnie's new lifestyle and reluctantly moved into the same boardinghouse. While Winnie's goal was to become independently wealthy so that she could travel and move to more exotic destinations, Suzanne's goal was to be able to start her own dress shop and become a successful businesswoman. She wanted to be like Austina with her bakery."

"Austina remained friends with the two young ladies in spite of their chosen profession. She wasn't the type of person to judge others or to look down on anyone. She still saw her friends as the sisters she never had."

"While Austina and Christopher were noble in their dealings with Suzanne and Winnie after they become ladies of ill fame, many in Memphis were not as welcoming. Austina's parents even advocated that she stop associating with people of such ungodly character. I was in the bakery one day and heard Austina respond in a manner calculated to appeal to her father's business sense: 'They eat baked goods just like a preacher or a priest.'"

The captain laughed to hear Austina's witty retort. He then suggested, "So, Suzanne and Winnie were the closest things to aunts that either of these boys ever had. Is that fair to say?"

"Well, I suppose you could say that. However, I need to point out that Winnie left town at some point in that week of exodus in '78. I once asked Suzanne why she didn't leave too. She just said the need was greater for her to stay and help where she could."

Taking notes of what he was being told delayed the captain from asking his next question. "So, Gunsie and Ira went to live in the brothel with Suzanne. How did that work out and how long did it last?"

Looking down to her clasped hands, she replied, "I only got limited information about the three of them after that. From what I heard, the boys finished up school and started working small jobs. They were both really good with horses and would care for them while the owners were visiting residents of the house. The arrangement only lasted a year. You see, in 1879, yellow fever returned. I was again dispatched to care for orphans out in Forest Hill. When I returned in November of that year, I learned that Suzanne had died of the fever while caring for others."

The captain slowly shook his head as he continued taking notes. He looked up and asked, "What happened to the boys after she died?"

Now it was Sister Margarete's turn to slowly shake her head. "I do not know for certain what became of them after that. I heard that Ira headed to the outlands to join the cavalry. Gunsie may have joined him as well. I just do not know for certain."

After quickly glancing over the notes he had taken, the captain asked, "What is the story behind Gunsie's nickname?"

Sister Margarete smiled and asked, "Do you mean, why was he called Cuz? Well, either Christopher or Ira gave him that name. I believe it had something to do with Christopher adopting Ira and then Ira not wanting to refer to Gunsie as his brother. Ira said he had a little brother and little sister who both died in the orphanage and out of respect for them, he just didn't want to call anyone else his brother. When Gunsie asked his father what he should say when asked about his relation to Ira, Christopher answered, 'Well, boys, in the big circle of life, we'ze all cousins.' Gunsie liked that and Ira started calling him Cuz from that time. Gunsie even enjoyed it when Suzanne and Winnie would call him Cuz since he never knew how to explain how he was related to them other than to say that they were all cousins."

The captain then zeroed in on his planned follow-up question. "What about Christopher? I know his records listed him as Luke. Why is that?"

With a tilt of her head, she answered, "I heard Suzanne call him Luke once. Later I asked him about it and he just told me it had something to do with the Gospel of Luke. Several months later, I saw Suzanne and she again referred to Christopher as Luke, so I asked her why. She appeared stunned that I didn't know. She then explained that Austina used to always call him that because of the situation that led to him losing his arm at Shiloh. Austina felt that if Christopher hadn't been a Good Samaritan to that wounded Yankee, he probably wouldn't have gotten shot himself. Since the parable of the Good Samaritan could only be found in the Gospel of Luke, Austina started calling him that."

Sensing no more girls would attempt to skip class, Sister Margarete stood and started walking back to the main entrance. "The thing about the reason for the nickname just seemed appropriate for him. He would always help people in need and never cared what anyone thought of it. Prostitutes, Catholics, black people, poor people, if he saw that they were in need, he'd stop and give assistance."

With a furrowed brow, he asked, "Did he have any other nicknames?"

She thought for a moment and just shook her head.

The captain then suggested, "Perhaps, because of his war injury, people would have called him Stumpy, or some other similar nickname."

"Oh, mercy, no!" she exclaimed. "Who would have been so terribly insensitive? Mocking a man's war wounds. How shameful!"

At least the captain now knew that Christopher was not the man Cuz claimed to have murdered. After apologizing for his previous question, he asked, "Do you know of anyone who went by the nickname Stumpy?"

Again, Sister Margarete answered, "No, I don't. Why is Stumpy important?"

"Well Sister Margarete, Gunsie firmly believes that he murdered some man named Stumpy and that is why he ran away from Memphis back in 1882. I seriously doubt it since he is suffering from malaria and prone to having wild nightmares and vivid delusions. However, Gunsie believes it to be true, and I'm hoping to find the evidence necessary to convince him he's no murderer."

She quickly dismissed the idea that Gunsie could have murdered anyone. However, she quickly did the math to realize that Gunsie had not left Memphis when Ira did.

She then asked, "Where did he live for the three years after Suzanne died and Ira left town?"

Frustrated, the captain said, "That's what I'm trying to find out. It seems the more I learn, the more questions I have."

"The boardinghouse where Suzanne lived when she took the boys in was over on Hill Street between Mosby and Concord, I believe. Not all of the residents are women of ill fame. Maybe someone around there will remember something."

The captain explained that he had a couple of people at the newspaper who were helping him research information that might produce some useful leads.

Arriving at the front entrance, Sister Margarete bid the captain farewell as she added, "I will light a candle for Gunsie and pray for his improved health. Good luck to you in your search. I hope you find the proof you need to convince him that he didn't murder anyone."

With a concerned look on his face, he responded, "What if I find out that he really did murder someone?"

Her quick response was, "You find the truth and leave the judging to God."

Snickering slightly, the captain said, "Funny—that's almost the same advice Colonel Dean gave me."

Chapter Four

Cynthia's House

The next stop of the day was to see Eli at the newspaper. After arriving there, the captain was pleased to hear that Eli had not yet seen J.B. to have her research the list of names they had developed the previous afternoon. Seeing the confusion on Eli's face, the captain explained, "I don't want to waste J.B.'s time since I already answered the questions we had. Specifically, Luke is Christopher's nickname, so they are one and the same person. I also learned that Ira was a friend of Gunsie's from the orphanage."

Eli replied, "Orphanage?"

Once they sat down in Eli's office, the captain relayed all the information he had learned from his visit to St. Agnes. As the captain read from his notes, Eli made notes of his own to give to J.B. The current task was to find out everything that they could on Suzanne Dugan and Winnie Clay, and any mention of a boy named Ira who was adopted by Christopher Hayes.

Once the captain completed his debriefing for Eli, he told Eli some of the stories Sister Margarete had told regarding the yellow fever epidemic. Eli nodded in agreement. "We had cases of yellow fever almost every year, I seem to recall. They say the first epidemic of the yellow plague was back in 1828 when a couple hundred folks died. The next time we had deaths of epidemic proportions was in 1855 when a few more than a couple hundred died. In 1867, the fever took over 500 folks. That started to get some attention, but being right after the war, most folks just ignored death, choosing rather to focus on their own life and circumstance."

Eli lit up his pipe as he leaned back in his chair as he said, "Folks couldn't ignore the yellow fever epidemic of 1873. They say nearly 5,000 people got sick, and 2,000 of those folks died. It was five years later when we had another epidemic of yellow fever. That Sister Margarete told you right. The city population was about 50,000 when the word spread that the fever was back. By the end of the second week, there were only about 19,000 left in the city, and 17,000 of them got sick. Over 5,100 died."

Taking a long draw on his pipe, he slowly exhaled. As he looked at the small cloud of smoke hovering above him, he said, "This was a dirty and smelly place back then. There was no sewer system, dead animals would just be left to rot in the streets, and private privies would frequently overflow into the pathways. Contributing to the stench was the Nicholson Pavement; you know what that was, don't you?"

The captain just shook his head as Eli continued, "They were wooden blocks that were soaked in creosote. Folks thought it was a good idea to pave the streets with them. People thought it would make us look modernized like those big eastern cities. Well, when those blocks started to decay, they let off a most foul smell! Between the decaying Nicholson Pavement, raw sewage, dead animals, and mountains of garbage in the streets, the Surgeon General of the United States called Memphis a national disgrace. Visitors reported back to their homes that they could smell us five miles away."

Eli continued to reminisce. "In September of 1878, the few people who were left in the city stayed indoors. The only people who went out were the collectors of the dead. With horse and wagon, they paraded up and down the streets yelling, 'Bring out your dead!' Bodies were quickly buried to try to reduce the risk of spreading the fever to others."

The captain asked, "What other steps were taken to fight the spread of the disease?"

"Most folks tried to keep the bad air away. Temperatures were up near 100, but to keep the bad air out, they'd close all of the windows and doors, and start a fire in their fireplace or just light their stoves. All the fires kept the bad air out. Then, when people died of the fever, their clothing and bedding were dragged out into the streets and burned."

Eli took his pipe from his mouth as he paused for a second. He then said solemnly, "Nothing seemed to work. There were 200 new deaths each day. Corpses were everywhere."

Leaning back in his chair, Eli spoke about the people who had tried to make a difference in combating yellow fever in Memphis. "They turned St. Mary's Episcopal school into a hospital. They turned St. Agnes Academy into a hospital; Annie Cook turned her brothel into a hospital. Hell, there were hospitals everywhere, and people just kept dying. Nurses came here from Illinois. The Howard Association brought doctors here from New Orleans, Mississippi, and back east. Episcopalian nuns came here from Peekskill, New York. Most all of them died too."

Pointing to the captain with his pipe, Eli said, "Did you know that Sister Constance of St. Mary's went from house to house to care for the sick? Sometimes she found abandoned children amid the rotting corpses of their parents. She took ill with yellow fever and died too. Priests, doctors, nurses, nuns, and prostitutes all tried to care for their sick neighbors regardless if they were friends or strangers—they all ended up in 'No Man's Land' over in Elmwood."

Seeing the slight look of confusion on the captain's face, Eli explained that the four mass burial trenches at Elwood Cemetery that had been set aside for victims of the yellow fever epidemic had been named No Man's Land.

"Yes, many people courageously stood their ground to help others. It earned them a lot of respect and forced us to re-evaluate the way we look at Catholics, blacks, and Irish. But I have to say I'm most impressed with the prostitutes!"

The captain was shocked to hear this statement and quickly blurted, "Really? Why is that?"

Eli again leaned forward in his chair as he said, "Think about their daily life. The men they serviced condemned their presence every other day of the week. The respectable women of this city vehemently condemned them, even spat at them in public. Some actually resorted to throwing tomatoes at these women of ill fame. Then, regardless of the way the citizenry treated them, these women turned their brothels into hospitals to care for the sick. Prostitutes like this Suzanne you were telling me about and others died nursing the very people who spat on them and ridiculed them just a few days earlier. Emily Sutton was another Memphis madam who died of yellow fever. I'm proud to say that I donated to the effort to give her a beautiful monument in Elmwood."

The captain thought about what Eli had said and then asked a rhetorical question. "What monuments were built to honor the 30 nuns who died while rendering aid to the citizenry? From what Sister Margarete tells me, most of them were laid to rest in a small cemetery right there on the grounds of St. Agnes Academy. No big monument exists to honor their sacrifice."

Eli quipped, "Would they've wanted a monument?"

Deciding to change the subject, the captain asked, "How did the epidemics change the way Memphians saw blacks?"

Eli became wide-eyed as he exclaimed, "They were the only law around! Before the '78 epidemic, Memphis had a sizable police force of over 40 men. When the fever hit, there were only seven left who were fit for duty. One by one, they died at their posts. The blacks stepped up and became policemen. As for the other areas of the city, they kept things working the best they could. Black folk worked as nurses, cart drivers, firemen, coffin makers, and gravediggers. It's only been in the past few months that our illustrious city officials have started pushing that blacks be banned from city employment. I dare say many of the powers to be who are pushing for that ban weren't here in the city after everyone else left."

Suddenly, the two men realized that J.B. was standing in the doorway awaiting her latest research assignment. While Eli and the captain stood prioritizing the list of questions they wanted answered, J.B. quietly stood in the doorway and stared at the floor near where the captain was standing. Eli carefully printed a list of names and words, and handed it to J.B. In an instant, she had left to start her research.

Realizing the time, the captain decided it was time to return to his mother-in-law's house. After all, it would be rude to be late for dinner.

Polly was in the front yard turning the soil in her mother's flower garden. Noticing the captain's arrival, she remarked, "Great, you're home early. You can change and help me out here before dinner's ready."

Hearing the conversation from inside the house, Lavinia opened the front door and said, "Hello, Daniel. Welcome back."

Knowing she was still waiting for him to call her by her first name, he disappointed her again when he replied, "Good afternoon, Mrs. Reiley. It's a beautiful day, isn't it?"

Lavinia just scoffed as she flashed a smile towards her daughter. Turning to go back inside, she said, "Dinner will be ready in an hour."

After working in the flower garden, the two houseguests cleaned up and sat down to dinner. Lavinia had fried up some bluegill she got from Mrs. Massey, the next-door neighbor. Evidently it was part of an elaborate bartering deal among five neighbors that involved fruit preserves, canned relish, a bottle of home-made balm wine, a large cornbread, and a quart of buttermilk. Lavinia was quite pleased with herself over the acquisition.

The captain told Polly and Lavinia all about his day, including his meeting with Sister Margarete and all the information he had learned about the yellow fever epidemics. Lavinia attempted to suggest that the conversation wasn't appropriate for the dinner table, but Polly was used to it. "Trust me, mother, this is far better than talking about horrible battle wounds and burned tissue. That's usually the type of dinner conversation we have."

He just rolled his eyes as he continued talking about how so many Memphians had left the city on such short notice and how courageous the people were who could've left but decided to stay behind and help where needed.

Realizing that her protests were futile, Lavinia contributed, "I will have you know that I am one of those people who picked up and left. I hope you don't think that I was being cowardly to leave. Polly was only 11 in 1878. I had to think of her health, didn't I?"

The captain immediately pointed out that in combat, some soldiers do courageous acts. This does not mean that soldiers who did not get recognized for courage under fire were cowards. He stressed to his mother-in-law that just because he was recognizing the nerve shown by the ones who stayed, he was in no way criticizing people for leaving. Obviously there was something in the city that was killing people, and the safest thing to do was to get as far away as possible.

He went on, "It was a very brave thing to walk away from your home and personal belongings for the safety of your family. Then, living in a refugee camp, surrounded by strangers and living in constant concern that the yellow fever would still find you. No, ma'am, I don't think that is cowardice at all."

Polly quipped, "Who knew that it may have been more pleasant talking about burned flesh?"

Lavinia blushed slightly, realizing she had been overly sensitive and misinterpreted what her son-in-law was implying. She said, "Yes, we did leave many valuables when we left, but they were all there when we returned. Mrs. Beaumont weren't so lucky—carpetbaggers cleaned her out before she got back!"

"You don't know that they were carpetbaggers who stole her things!" Polly exclaimed.

"Indeed I do know! The scoundrel tried to sell her things back to her at twice what she paid for them in the first place."

The captain asked, "Did she notify the police?"

Lavinia sat up straight in her chair and answered, "She tried to report it, but when that black fellow in the police uniform showed up, she refused to speak to him. I told her that it was nonsense to not report that low-life carpetbagger for what he'd done just because the policeman was a black man. She just told me that she'd lived to be 67 years old and survived wars, disease, two husbands, five children, and poverty without never talking to a black man, and she weren't about to start now."

Polly and her husband glanced at each other in shock as they both commented on how terrible it was that the thief would get away with his crimes just because Mrs. Beaumont wouldn't speak to a black man.

Polly asked, "Where was the refugee camp that we went to?"

Lavinia explained, "It's just outside a little community called Ridgeway just past White's Station."

Polly asked, "Can the three of us go out there to see it? Maybe it'd bring back better memories of the time."

The captain agreed, saying, "It'll be a nice ride in the country."

The next morning, Wednesday, was the twenty-second day of March. After a filling breakfast of delicious biscuits and gravy, the captain headed out to follow up on the leads Sister Margarete had given him. First on his agenda was to go to the last known address of Suzanne Dugan since this was also the last known address for Gunsie before he abruptly left town.

The only location he had for the boardinghouse was Hill Street between Mosby and Concord. When he got there, he found several boardinghouses with no clear indication as to which one could have been Gunsie's temporary home. With a determined sigh, he stood tall and began asking people as they came and went.

After 20 minutes of this tedious task, he finally received some promising direction from one elderly man who seemed to remember a Miss Suzy and two young teenagers living at Lolla's house.

As the captain got close, he noticed a middle-aged lady with her bust bulging from her low-cut dress sweeping the front porch. "Excuse me, ma'am. Is this Lolla's house?"

Tersely, she replied, "Not since she headed out to the western outlands 10 years ago. It's my place now." As she looked up from her sweeping to finally notice the captain, her tone changed, "Well, hello there, general! It's a little early in the day for my girls to be receiving visitors but I'm sure we can arrange something to please you."

The captain nervously laughed as he blushed. "I'm sure it would be a most satisfying experience; however, I'm here on official business."

Propping her broom in the corner, she said, "General, we can make it our business to make you forget about your business."

With a slight stammer, he replied, "Yes, ma'am. I'm sure you could..."

"Please, everyone calls me Miss Cynthia," she said as she stepped closer to her slightly flustered guest.

Clearing his throat quickly, he tried again to state his purpose for being there. "Yes, ma'am...uh...Miss Cynthia, I'm Captain Hodges, and I'm looking for..."

Cynthia interrupted, "Well, captain, honey, we're all looking for someone special."

Summoning a firmer tone, he continued again. "I'm looking for anyone who may have known Suzanne Dugan or the two boys she took in." Noticing Miss Cynthia was still looking at him as if she were hungry and he was an apple cobbler, he added, "It would've been around 1878 or 1879."

Cynthia placed a hand on her hip and sighed disappointedly as she said, "Cairy may have been here back then. She may remember some of the folks who lived here when it was still Miss Lolla's."

"May I speak to her?"

Miss Cynthia protested, "It's too early! My ladies need their beauty rest, so they can look their best for their guests."

As Miss Cynthia started to suggest that he should return in the late afternoon, the front door flew open and out came a tall blonde-haired lady hurriedly tying her robe. "Why are you asking about Cuz and Ira?" she urgently asked. "I heard you through my cracked window over there."

Stepping forward, the captain asked, "Did you know Cuz?"

Checking again to ensure her robe had been securely tied, she replied, "Yes, I knew him. I was about 10 when Miss Suzy brought him and his friend Ira here to live. Do you know Cuz? Is he well?"

Miss Cynthia interjected, "This is Miss Cairy, general."

The captain explained Cuz's situation and why he wanted to find out more about his last days in Memphis.

Miss Cynthia, realizing this wasn't going to be a brief visit, brought the captain into the front parlor where they could be more comfortable. Once they were situated, Miss Cairy explained how she met the boys. "After my maw died of consumption, I had no place to go 'cept here to live with my Aunt Tampe. She was good friends with Miss Suzy and Miss Win. They was both real nice ladies, but especially

Miss Suzy. She taught me some read'n and even some numbers. She used to always tell me a girl's got to know stuff if they wanna follow their dreams. She had dreams of making dresses for fancy women. She said she was gonna take me with her when she left."

Sitting up straight and refocusing on the captain's original question, Miss Cairy continued, "One day, Miss Suzy brought these two boys home with her from the hospital and said they was orphans and had no place else to go. So they stayed here. Well, at least most of the time. On busy nights, they'd send us young'uns to the loft at the stables for the night. You know, Ira used to work there? It wasn't so bad there. The horses were much quieter than some of the men who would come calling. Cuz and Ira took care of me like I was their little sister. Ira once told me he used to have a little sister and that I reminded him of her. He never said what happened to her."

The captain said, "Miss Suzy died of yellow fever during the 1879 epidemic. What happened to the boys after that?"

Miss Cairy quickly responded. "Cuz went next door to live with Miss Annie and Miss Jess. Ira said he was too old to be live'n off of others and left. I never saw him again."

The captain asked, "This Miss Annie and Miss Jess, were they prostitutes next door?"

Miss Cairy laughed as she exclaimed, "Oh dear lord, no. They was widows who lived next door. They was right fine folks, both of 'em." After Ira left, the owner of the stables wouldn't let us stay in the loft anymore. The widows took Cuz in and let me stay there whenever my room got too noisy."

While Miss Cynthia continued to usher curious ladies away from the parlor, the captain continued his question-ing. "When was the last time you saw Cuz?"

"The last time I saw Cuz was Independence Day, 1882. The widows were going to take me to see the fireworks down by the river. Cuz said he was going to meet us there, but he never did. When we got back home, Miss Jess said she was going to go look for him. Later, when she came back without him, Miss Annie said she was going to go look for him. We never saw him again. He just up and vanished. It broke my heart that he'd leave without even saying goodbye. I know we was just kids, but I was kind of sweet on him."

The captain was excited to be able to narrow down Cuz's last day in Memphis to July 4, 1882. He even asked Miss Cairy to verify the date before writing down what he just learned. When he finished, he looked up and asked Miss Cairy, "Who was Stumpy?"

Before Miss Cairy could answer, Miss Cynthia turned from her sentry post at the parlor door and blurted, "If you are friends with Stumpy, I'll ask you to leave this house at once! No friend of his is welcome here."

Remaining in his seat, the captain firmly stated, "I am not friends with Stumpy. I don't even know who he is. However, I can assume that you are aware of who he is."

Miss Cairy and Miss Cynthia exchanged glances before Miss Cynthia replied, "Yes, we knew the little worm! He was the lowest form of vermin in this city. A vile and despicable carpetbagger who never met a person that he didn't try to steal from."

Miss Cairy spoke up. "Miss Win was Stumpy's favorite girl, but she stopped seeing him on account he never paid when he should've. He always wanted to pay her next time. Miss Win put her foot down and said there won't be a next time. Miss Lolla supported the decision and banned Stumpy from her house. Stumpy was furious and made a big scene whenever he couldn't see Miss Win."

Miss Cynthia interjected, "That's when the snake bamboozled Miss Lolla out of her other boardinghouse over on High Street. During the yellow fever epidemics of '78 and '79 Stumpy was so busy stealing property from fever victims he didn't bother with the brothels much and didn't realize Miss Lolla had just moved over here. Once Stumpy found out that Miss Win had vanished, he demanded to know where she went. When nobody would tell him anything, he got enraged again and went after Miss Lolla's house again. Just as he was about to hoodwink some fellows over at the bank to foreclose on her, she and I made a deal to put the house in my name. That caused enough confusion to stall him."

The captain continued to take notes before looking at both ladies and asking, "Do you know what this man's name was and why everyone called him Stumpy?"

Both ladies chuckled as they twinkled their eyes before explaining. "Honey, in our business, we don't call nobody by their true name. Sometimes they give us the nickname they want us to know them by and then other times..."

Both ladies snickered slightly again before Miss Cairy said, "Many times, we give them nicknames from our first impressions of them. Like there's Stop-watch, Doggie, Locust, and Dough-man..."

Interrupting, Miss Cynthia added, "Of course, our preferred guests have more impressive names, such as Hickory, Hercules, Rock, and Longbow." Looking seductively at the captain, she added, "I bet we'd end up calling you Tiger, wouldn't we?"

The captain quickly continued his questioning. "So, everybody knew this guy as Stumpy? Didn't anyone know his real name?"

Miss Cynthia, still smiling from being able to fluster the captain, said, "I may still have a letter in my desk from Stumpy's lawyer."

She left to find it while Miss Cairy continued talking about nicknames. "You know, they called him Cuz because he always said we was all cousins?" The captain nodded as she continued, "They called Ira Horse because he...uh...well, he worked in the stables."

She nervously blushed and laughed slightly before asking, "When you see Cuz, will you tell him I was asking about him?"

As the captain was agreeing to relay the message to Cuz, Miss Cynthia entered the room with a piece of paper in her hand. "Clarence Green Vendig, that's the swindler's name."

Writing down the name on his notepad, he asked, "I take it that this Mr. Vendig didn't like his nickname too much?"

"He loathed it! The more he protested, the more folks would use the name just to rile him."

"Did he have a wife or family?"

Miss Cynthia again looked at him seductively and replied, "Suga, ain't nobody married or have kids when they come through those doors."

The captain responded, "Yes, I see what you mean. Well, whatever happened to the widows?"

Miss Cairy answered, "Miss Annie came into some money soon after Cuz vanished. So, she and Miss Jess got themselves a nice home of their own out in the country somewhere around East Parkway and Central Avenue. I guess they're still there. I haven't heard from them in quite a spell."

Looking back over his notes, the captain thought that he had enough leads to keep him busy for the next few days. Knowing now who Stumpy was, the captain could not understand Cuz's connection to him, much less why he would want to do the man any harm. With an inquisitive look, he asked, "Did Cuz know Stumpy?"

The two ladies slowly shook their heads and said, "We weren't aware that Cuz even knew Stumpy."

Miss Cynthia then looked as if she remembered something and said, "He may have witnessed a few of the dustups Stumpy caused from the sidewalk. Not too many folks could have missed hearing those."

The captain thanked the ladies for their time. As he was leaving, Miss Cynthia couldn't resist saying, "You come back real soon. All right, Tiger?"

He didn't get to the newspaper office until early afternoon. He and Eli quickly updated one another. J.B. had been busy finding articles that contained any reference to the list of names she'd been given. Eli placed the archived newspapers on an empty desk in the outer offices and invited the captain to delve into J.B.'s findings.

After two hours of reading and taking notes, the captain had completed his task. Returning to Eli's office with one of the archived newspapers, he said, "Eli, I believe I dis-covered a mistake that J.B. committed. I've gone over this referenced page four times, and none of the names we gave her are here."

"Open the paper on my desk so we can both look." After a minute, Eli started laughing and asked, "Man, don't you see?"

The captain shook his head.

Eli pointed to an advertisement for the Louis Department Store as he exclaimed, "It's your boots! She saw these boots and thought that since you were wearing the same ones that they should be on the list."

Still amazed, the captain continued to look at the picture of the boots in disbelief. Finally, he apologized to Eli for thinking J.B. had made a mistake. He then worked with him in creating a new list of questions they had from the day's activities.

First, they wanted to track down the widows to ask them what they knew about Cuz and Stumpy. Second, now that they knew Stumpy's real name, they needed to look for anything they could learn about him and why anyone, especially Cuz, may have wanted him dead. Lastly, Eli was very interested in Stumpy's property foreclosure scam. How was he able to take over Lolla's house and who else was he able to kick to the streets?

Returning home, the captain was happy that Lavinia hadn't made a point of trying to get him to call her by her first name. Once he and Polly had caught one another up on their day's activities, they joined Lavinia for dinner. They were having fried chicken and mashed potatoes. The captain felt like a pig asking for seconds, but the chicken was so delicious that he couldn't help himself.

Afterwards, they sat in the front parlor as they sipped on George's home-made currant wine. The captain found it even more robust than last night's wine. Lavinia and Polly smiled and stared out of the window as they drank their wine. As it turned out, it was an early evening for them all.

Chapter Five

The Widows

Early Thursday morning, a knock on the front door interrupted the captain's breakfast. Upon answering the door, he met a young lad from *The Scimitar*. Thinking that he was there to collect for Lavinia's newspaper delivery, the captain started to retrieve his wallet to pay. However, the boy called out, "Would you be Captain Hodge?"

Surprised, the captain acknowledged his identity and asked how he could help him.

The messenger handed the captain an envelope and said, "Mr. Nuttal asked that I bring this to you right away."

The captain appreciated the boy's professionalism and offered a monetary token of appreciation. However the boy ardently refused the tip, saying, "Mr. Nuttal already took care of my fee."

The captain replied, "Of course. But is there something I can offer to express my thanks?"

The boy sheepishly looked over his shoulder before saying "A bottle of Mr. Reiley's wine would be greatly appreciated sir."

The captain laughed as he informed the lad, "I'm not even sure I'm old enough to be drinking his wine!"

The boy thanked the captain nonetheless before riding off.

The note contained the address for the widows out on East Parkway. Excited to have received the information, he hurriedly finished breakfast and headed directly there.

Arriving at the specified address, the captain recalled what Miss Cairy had said about one of the widows having come into some money. From the looks of it, there was quite a bit of money involved. While not extravagant, the home was considerably more comfortable than living in the boardinghouses.

Walking up to the front door, he was still admiring the residential setting when he heard, "Well, it's about time you showed up!" Startled, he noticed an older lady turning the soil in the flower beds. She turned towards the house and yelled, "Jess! That man the church said they were sending over is here!"

The captain tried to correct her assumption and introduce himself when Miss Jess appeared at the front door and hollered out, "You sure took your sweet time getting here! Come on in here, these boxes ain't gonna move themselves. I do declare I never thought it'd take you six months to get here!"

The captain tried again to clarify the misunderstanding, but Miss Annie interrupted him by yelling at Jess. "It ain't been six months! Christmas was only three months ago."

Jess replied, "Six months or three months—don't matter, the preacher promised he'd send someone right over, and we've been tripping over these boxes all this time."

Annie continued to turn the soil as she said, "When you're done with the boxes, there's a spare shovel over here for you to start on that other flower bed."

As the captain tried once more to clarify his purpose, Jess squawked, "Come along, young man. These boxes are right through yonder."

By now, the captain accepted the fact that he was going to move some boxes and work in the flower bed before he was going to get any information out of either of these widows. As it turned out, the boxes were Christmas decorations that had been sitting in the hallway. The widows must have had some difficulty squeezing through the small opening in the hallway to get to the back of the house. It was no wonder they were so anxious to have them moved to the attic.

Once he had moved the boxes, Miss Jess offered him a glass of water. Taking a gulp, he quickly heard Miss Annie from outside yelling, "Ain't that young man finished with them boxes yet? This shovel is rust'n up wait'n on him!"

Miss Jess reached out and took the glass away from the captain as she smiled and pointed towards the door. "Hurry along now, you don't want to keep her waiting. You need to get started before she starts using her motivational vocabulary. She does know quite a few of those words, and we'll all be happier if we don't hear any of them this morning, don't you know?"

Playing along with the ambush, the captain grabbed the shovel and started tilling the dirt. The fact that he had helped Polly work the flower beds only a couple of nights before helped the captain's performance meet Miss Annie's approval. When he was about half-way through the current task, he told Miss Annie, "You know that the church didn't send me over here to do your chores, don't you?"

Wiping her forehead quickly, she replied, "Don't care who sent you—chores got to get done."

The captain worked a little more before asking, "Didn't you wonder why I'm wearing an army uniform?"

Without looking up, Miss Annie replied, "After the war, a lot of men continued to wear their uniforms on account of they couldn't afford nothing else. What you wear to work in don't concern me none."

As he finished turning the soil, Miss Jess came out of the house and stood on the front porch.

Deciding to take a different approach in dealing with the widows, he asked, "Do you remember Gunsie Hayes?"

Almost in unison, the widows responded. "Cuz? You know Cuz?"

Now it was the captain's turn to play coy as he delayed his response while turning over the last few sections of the flower bed.

Miss Annie stood up and asked, "How do you know Cuz? Is he all right? Where is he? Will he be coming here soon?"

Miss Jess looked on anxiously awaiting the captain's response.

Turning the last bit of the flower bed, the captain jabbed the shovel into the dirt and finally introduced himself. After he told the widows the reason of his visit, they asked him to sit on the porch and ask his questions.

Miss Jess began asking several questions in rapid succession. "How is Cuz doing? Where's he been all these years? Is he married? Does he have any children?"

Miss Annie barked, "Jess! Let the man speak. I'm sure he'll get around to answering your questions at some point."

The captain began by clarifying, "Just so I understand, Cuz moved in with you after Miss Suzy died. Is that right?"

Miss Annie nodded while she folded her arms, allowing Miss Jess to answer. "Yes. That's right. Miss Suzy was the real nice harlot that worked at the brothel next door to where we was living. She tried to care for Cuz and that other boy. What was his name?"

Miss Annie tersely replied, "Ira. He was a fine lad too."

Miss Jess nodded as she continued, "Yes, Ira was his name. Those boys had a rough go of it in their early years. Miss Suzy wasn't in the best position to care for two young boys, you know, working in a brothel and such. But her heart was pure gold. She saw to it that those boys were well fed and had decent clothes and ..."

Miss Annie interrupted. "Yes, Cuz moved in with us after Miss Suzy died. Only Cuz moved in—Ira ran off saying he was too old to depend on others."

"When was the last time either of you saw Cuz?"

Miss Jess shook her head slowly as she tried to remember. Meanwhile, Miss Annie bluntly replied, "It was 5 July, 1882."

Miss Jess added, "Yes, it was the day after the fireworks. Has it really been that long ago?"

The captain looked at both ladies and asked, "Did he tell either of you why he was leaving?"

The widows looked at each other briefly before Miss Annie replied, "No. He didn't come home the night before, and then when he showed up the next morning, he grabbed some of his things and left. We called out for him to tell us what was going on, but he never stopped."

"And neither of you have heard from him since?"

Both ladies shook their heads.

The captain told the little he knew about Cuz's movements since he left Memphis: his career in the army, his battle record in the Indian Wars out West, and the Spanish-American War in Cuba. "Malaria is causing Cuz to have some bad nightmares about his life in Memphis."

Miss Annie quipped, "It was probably over Jess' cooking!"

Miss Jess smiled, giggled slightly, and added, "I never was able to cook spotted gar without burning it for some reason."

"Oh, no, ma'am, these nightmares have nothing to do with either of you ladies or your cooking. It seems that Cuz is convinced that he murdered some man by the name of Clarence Green Vendig. Only, Cuz referred to him as Stumpy."

The widows quickly looked at one another as if the captain had hit a nerve. Miss Annie looked over the yard quickly and then suggested that the three of them go inside to continue their discussion.

As the three of them got settled in the parlor and Miss Jess served water, the captain asked, "Why would Cuz believe that he murdered Stumpy?"

Miss Jess spilled a little water as he asked the question. She fumbled briefly as she tried to clean up her mess.

Miss Annie confidently answered, "Cuz didn't kill nobody, especially that cow-turd of an excuse for a man!"

Miss Jess gasped at her friend's vulgar description. "Annie! You know I don't approve of such filthy language to be used in my presence!"

Miss Annie nodded her head and said, "I won't be apologizing for saying what's what! The captain here needs to know what a miserable person Stumpy was."

Miss Jess smiled at their guest and added, "You know, he really hated being called Stumpy? The painted ladies called him that on account of..."

Miss Annie interrupted to say, "Stumpy was stabbed to death by some fellows he tried to swindle. At least, that's the story we heard."

"Why would Cuz think he murdered this guy then?"

Miss Annie quickly replied, "Twern't no reason for Cuz to kill Stumpy or nobody else!"

Miss Jess started to speak, but Miss Annie gave her a stern look that froze her tongue.

The captain jotted a couple of notes and then asked, "How did you ladies know Stumpy?"

Miss Jess sat back in her chair, clearly not wanting to say the wrong thing after Miss Annie's previous look.

Miss Annie answered, "That rascal would stand on the street yelling and cursing on account he'd been banned from Lolla's House. We was right next door—we saw it all! Then he went off and tried to take over all the boardinghouses on the block just to run Miss Lolla out of business. He was an evil and villainous excuse of a man!"

Miss Jess added, "Set on revenge, he was!"

Miss Annie nodded and said, "All on account of his favorite girl stopped taking his worthless IOUs for services rendered. Good for her, I say!"

Miss Jess nodded firmly.

"So Miss Lolla must've not liked Stumpy too much."

Miss Jess quickly replied, "Oh, she threatened to kill him a few times."

With another disapproving glance at her friend, Miss Annie added, "The point is, that snake caused a lot of decent folks to have to leave their homes all cause he couldn't be with his favorite harlot. That means that there were many folks who wanted to see Stumpy dead. Not just Miss Lolla—and certainly not Cuz!"

Standing to leave, the captain thanked the widows for their help. Miss Jess thanked him for moving the boxes to the attic before Miss Annie said, "Yeah, thanks. I guess I've seen worse flower beds before."

Walking to the door, Miss Jess asked inquisitively, "Are you married?"

He replied, "Yes. I am happily married to a wonderful lady. We are currently staying at her mother's house."

Miss Jess smiled as she said, "Oh, so you married a Memphis lady, how sweet. What is her name? Maybe we know her family."

Miss Annie rolled her eyes before the captain could answer. "My wife's maiden name was Polly Heaston. Her mother remarried, and her name is now Mrs. Lavinia Reiley."

Both widows glanced quickly at one another before clarifying that Lavinia was married to George Reiley. Once they realized they knew Lavinia, Miss Annie smiled for the first time as she asked, "By chance do you know if George has bottled any more of that delicious currant wine?"

The captain laughed. "How do you know about George's wine-making hobby?"

Miss Jess covered her mouth. "I won a bottle on a raffle ticket I bought at the women's auxiliary meeting."

Miss Annie added, "It was the strongest...uh, I mean, most flavorful currant wine we've had."

"I'll send you a bottle if there's still one available!"

There was still time for him to check in with Eli at the paper to see if they had uncovered any more information about Stumpy. As soon as he entered, Eli called out from his back office. "Captain! It's about time you got here. We've got all kinds of information to tell you about."

As soon as they got settled in Eli's office, he started sharing information that J.B. had found on Clarence Green Vendig. "It appears that nearly everyone in this town wanted Stumpy dead, and that includes your boy Cuz."

The captain was disappointed that Eli had found a possible motive for Cuz to have actually killed Stumpy. He had started to hope that Cuz was actually innocent after the widows' reassurances.

Eli explained, "First of all, Stumpy was the man who killed Cuz's mother. There's your first motive for why the boy wanted Stumpy dead. Then, when I was looking into all of Stumpy's land swindles, I found that one of the homes he absconded with belonged to Christopher Hayes, Cuz's father. Now, as if all of this wasn't enough reason for Cuz to go after this scallywag, Stumpy had also caused the evictions of Miss Lolla and the widows, who had all given Cuz a roof over his head."

Shaking his head, the captain admitted, "These are three clear motives for Cuz to have killed Stumpy."

Eli added, "However, like I said earlier, there were plenty of others who wanted Stumpy dead. Besides your boy, Cuz, and the widows, and the prostitutes from Miss Lolla's, there are several people he either directly or indirectly stole from. He blackmailed bankers, political figures. Hell, there's even one judge we know for a fact was in his pocket! Then there's the gamblers he owed money to…"

The captain interjected, "Most gamblers can't collect money from a dead man."

Eli smiled and said, "Most riverboat gamblers who come to town for a game care more about principles and reputation than actually collecting a delinquent account."

Shaking his head slowly, the captain admitted to Eli that Cuz still looked good for Stumpy's murder.

Eli held his hand up and said, "Well, hold up a bit because there's more. There were several folks who were looking to sell property to the county for a new courthouse. They were looking to collect a handsome profit off the deal."

The captain quickly asked, "So, what happened?"

Eli said, "Stumpy was arrested for Austina's murder. While awaiting arraignment, he was visited by several political figures. Then, after about a week, the prosecutor announced that Austina's death was a terrible accident, and Stumpy was released from jail."

Shaking his head in disgust, Eli finished telling the story of the unbelievable tragedy. "Shortly after Stumpy was released, the county announced the acquisition of several acres upon which they would begin construction of their new courthouse. While officials deny any connection, it still appears that Stumpy bought his release by giving the county the property. All the other property owners who were looking to sell their property to the county were furious."

Eli further explained that while Stumpy had been released, the prostitutes still told everyone that would listen that he had murdered Austina. After all, Austina and Christopher were friends of theirs. Miss Win and Miss Suzy both were very vocal about Stumpy's guilt.

In retaliation, Stumpy started a campaign of harassment against the prostitutes in general, and Miss Win specifically, that lasted over the next several years. He even bought Lolla's house of ill fame and evicted everyone just for spite. The harassment continued even after the girls set up shop in another boardinghouse until finally Win left town to start fresh elsewhere.

The captain was still disappointed since it appeared Cuz had the best motive for killing Stumpy.

Eli then asked, "Hey, didn't Cuz have a friend named Ira?"

The captain nodded as he added, "Christopher took a boy named Ira in when he brought Cuz back home out of the orphanage."

"That's what I thought. Well, this may be just a bizarre coincidence, but J.B. found this personal ad about a man named Clarence Green Vendig and his three children: Ira, Sara, and J.J. It seems some lady was looking for the children. Now, I doubt there were two Clarence Green Vendigs, but this Ira guy they mention would have only been a year or two older than Cuz. It seems worth further investigation to find out if these two Iras are one and the same."

The captain started speculating. "So you think Cuz's friend Ira could also be Stumpy's son? Would he have a stronger motive for killing his father, if this turns out to be the same Ira, or does that just increase Cuz's motivation to kill Stumpy for abandoning his friend in an orphanage?"

Eli just shrugged his shoulders as he said, "We'll just have to see what we can turn up."

As the two men stood to leave, Eli patted the captain on the back, and with a smile, said, "You know, my life had become fairly dull until you came to town. Now, we're investigating multiple mysteries. Isn't this exciting?"

The captain smirked as he offered a correction. "Perhaps frustrating would be a better description."

Eli boisterously laughed as he replied, "Nonsense! The other day, you didn't even know Stumpy's real name. Now, you've been meeting with harlots, nuns, and little old widow ladies. I call that real progress!"

Chapter Six

Gayoso House Hotel

For dinner, the captain made reservations to take Polly to the posh Gayoso House Hotel downtown. They really hadn't had much time alone with each other since they arrived in Memphis, and he thought this would be a nice change of pace. As the young couple entered the lobby on their way to the restaurant, they were greeted by a familiar voice.

"Hello, Polly and Daniel. I wasn't sure how long I would have to wait for your arrival."

Polly immediately replied, "Mother! What are you doing here?"

The captain simply said, "Good afternoon, Mrs. Reiley. This is a surprise finding you here."

Lavinia just shook her head at his stubborn refusal not to call her Lavinia. She then smiled and said, "I just couldn't miss an opportunity to dine here. With George being away in Texas, when would I ever have a better chance to come here? I do hope you don't mind my joining you after all of the meals I have been so willing to prepare for you both while you stay with me."

Polly just gave her mother a disapproving look, while the captain had no option. "Please join us for dinner, Mrs. Reiley."

As they got situated at their table, the three commented on the signs of deterioration of the hotel. Once the pride of Memphis, the hotel used to be known up and down the Mississippi River for its service and elegance. However, now it appeared it was heavily worn and in need of refurbishment.

Through dinner, the captain started discussing the progress he had been making with his investigation. As soon as he mentioned Clarence Green Vendig's name, Lavinia interjected, "That man is an award-winning scoundrel if ever I knew one!"

With a stunned expression, the captain asked, "How do you know this man?"

Lavinia sat up straight and immediately clarified, "I didn't say I knew him but I do know of him. He had some peculiar nickname: Grumpy, Dumpy, Frumpy..."

The captain said, "Folks called him Stumpy."

"Yes! That's him. We were at the same yellow fever camp outside of town back in 1878. Typical carpetbagger! He quickly set up shop and began charging exorbitant prices for any supplies he could locate. While he was profiting from these displaced families, he was foreclosing on any tenants who failed to keep up payments. Then he began acquiring several homes and property from bank and tax auctions."

"After a few weeks, one of the young ladies in the camp caught his eye. He pursued her even though she was half his age and she fervently declined his advances. Maureen Arnold was her name. Anyway, he found out that her parents were losing their home to foreclosure. Well, I tell you, this was exactly the bait he needed to scheme another one of his plans."

"In no time at all, Maureen's father quickly agreed to Stumpy's suggestion to arrange for Maureen and him to get married in exchange for saving their home from seizure by the bank. Maureen was furious that she had been bartered off like livestock in exchange for a refinancing loan. Needless to say, it was a relationship that started out stormy and progressively deteriorated from that point."

The captain was still a little stunned that his mother-in-law actually knew Stumpy. Nonetheless, he arranged his thoughts and asked, "Did Maureen stay in the area after Stumpy died?"

Lavinia said that she didn't know whatever happened to either one of them after they left the camp. However, she added, "Maureen grew so callous in just those couple of months of marriage that she showed no emotion at all when Stumpy went ahead and foreclosed on her parents home. They ended up with nothing, but Maureen didn't want any more to do with them."

Polly gasped, "That is horrible! I cannot imagine people being so cruel."

The captain asked Lavinia, "By chance did you know if Stumpy was ever married before marrying Maureen?"

She just shook her head as she pointed out a light fixture on the wall that was hanging by a thread. "I wish you both could have seen this place before the war. It was truly magnificent back then."

The captain turned to Polly and said, "I'll have to see what I can find out about Maureen. It sounds like she may have hated Stumpy enough to kill him."

Lavinia, taking a small break from sipping her coffee, interjected, "Honey, I can tell you that most of the folks in that fever camp wanted to kill him!"

The captain became more perplexed by the ever-growing list of suspects, yet still not sufficiently discounting the possibility that Cuz had committed the crime as he so firmly believed.

The following morning was Friday, March 24. The captain headed directly to the police station for more information. He was happy to see that Allen Vickery, the police sergeant he had met previously, was on duty.

"You're back! Now, let me think...Captain Daniel Hodge. That's your name, right?"

"I'm impressed you remembered it from our brief meeting so many days ago, in light of all the people you must meet here on a daily basis."

"As I remember, you were asking about a suspicious death that may have occurred over 15 years ago."

"Sergeant Vickery, you have a keen memory!"

"Please, just call me Sarge like everybody else. Now, what brings you in this morning?"

The captain pulled out his notes and then asked what Sarge could tell him about Clarence Green Vendig and his involvement in the death of a lady by the name of Austina Hayes.

Sarge's face became serious as he turned to grab a book of records. "Mrs. Hayes died in what, 1867?"

The captain replied, "I'm showing that she died in November 1868."

Sarge plopped a book on the counter and began thumbing through the pages. Once he found the incident, something else caught his eye. He asked the captain's patience for a moment. Sarge left the area hollering, "Hey! Is Frank Mann still here? He hasn't left yet, has he?"

Shortly, Sarge returned to the office accompanied by a well-dressed elderly gentleman. "Captain Hodge, I would like to introduce you to Mr. Frank Mann. As luck would have it, he visits the station every Friday."

After the captain and Mr. Mann exchanged greetings, Sarge further explained. "Mr. Mann is now retired; however, he was the desk sergeant who recorded the death of Mrs. Hayes."

Excitedly, the captain asked Mr. Mann, "Do you remember the particular incident?"

Sarge positioned the ledger so that he could refresh his memory.

Mr. Mann's smile turned into a frown as he pushed the book away. "Yes, I remember that whole tragedy. I don't need to look at any notes since it is burned into my mind. The whole situation was a shameful turn of events."

Sarge provided a chair so that he could sit while he retold the story.

"Mrs. Hayes, you see, had been lifelong friends with a couple of harlots over in one of the boardinghouses. While she wasn't a prostitute herself, she didn't allow her friends' chosen profession to interfere with their friendship. Well, one afternoon, Mrs. Hayes was walking home, and this drunk ill-mannered man began making inappropriate advances towards her. Witnesses all said that she politely but firmly rejected the man. However, he wasn't the type to take no for an answer, so he persisted and grabbed her arm. She broke free and ran towards a house for help. As she ascended the concrete step to the front door, the drunk man grabbed her again, pulling her backwards. She lost her footing and fell hard on her head. The trauma to her head was too great, and she died the following morning."

After sipping some water Sarge had provided, Mr. Mann continued. "Thanks to the quick actions of neighbors, the drunk was located and arrested."

He paused and shook his head slowly before he said, "Since the drunk was a well-known carpetbagger with deep ties to the federal puppet government, the charge of murder was reduced to disorderly public conduct. Mrs. Hayes' death was ruled an unfortunate accident. Can you believe that? We had witnesses who saw that reprobate attack that fine lady. And then he attacked her as she fled for safety. But the federals said it was a misunderstanding and that it was nothing more than a terrible accident."

Mr. Mann looked directly at the captain and asked, "You know she was a mother? She had a son. He was only five or six as I remember. But her killer was set free, and the county got the property for a new courthouse."

Sarge spoke up. "I heard about this story. I never knew the specifics until now." He looked at the book and then said, "Just to clarify for the captain, the killer was Clarence Green Vendig, is that correct?"

Mr. Mann nodded as the captain quickly asked, "Do you know whatever happened to Mr. Vendig?"

Mr. Mann thought about the question for a moment before answering. "Folks were filing charges against that slimy snake all the time. It seemed to be an endless stream of allegations of him bamboozling one person or another out of something. He always slithered out of it somehow. Then, well, he either found religion or skipped town, because around 1882 all complaints about him stopped."

Sarge figured that this might have been the unsolved murder the captain was asking about on his first visit. The captain saw the look on his face as he asked Mr. Mann, "He could have been murdered, don't you think?"

Mr. Mann slyly snickered with a wink as he answered, "You know what? Some men need killing!" He then sat up straight and added, "Actually, I'd be willing to bet that you couldn't find a single person who liked the man. While we are talking about money, I wish I had a nickel for every person you find who would have liked to see him dead!"

Sarge asked the captain, "What do you know about Mr. Vendig's death?"

The captain answered, "Nothing, really. I just learned what Stumpy's real name was the other day."

Mr. Mann laughed. "Stumpy! That's right! The folks used to call him that. Let me tell you, he really hated that nickname." He continued to laugh as he stood up to leave. After shaking hands, he thanked them for allowing him to be part of whatever investigation they were working on.

After Mr. Mann left, Sarge looked at the captain. Sensing he was about to ask again what he knew about Stumpy's death, the captain preemptively said, "All I know is that one person told me he died from a hit to his head and another told me he died in a barroom knife fight. I guess I'm just curious what really happened to him."

Sarge did not look convinced, but asked the captain to keep him briefed on any new information he learned about the matter. Meanwhile, he'd look through the records to see if he could find any information on Mr. Vendig's death now that he had more to go on than just his nickname.

The captain said, "Thank you. It would be helpful if you could find any records about it." He then flipped through his notes and added, "I was told that he had married a lady by the name of Maureen. Do you have any means to tell me where she might be living now?"

After flipping through a couple of books, Sarge offered an address for a Maureen Liguori as he said, "This lady has the same first name and is currently living at the last address I can find for Clarence Green. It might be the same Maureen, or it could just be a coincidence."

The captain thanked him for all of his assistance and promised to keep him informed about his findings.

Wasting no time, the captain hurried to the address he was given for Maureen in hopes that she was indeed Stumpy's widow. Once there, he was promptly confronted with a brusque greeting from the woman at the door.

After verifying the address one more time, the captain asked, "Are you Maureen Liguori?"

"Yes, why?"

"Were you married to Clarence Green Vendig?"

"You'll have to go to hell to collect any debts he owed you!" she said as she started to close the door on the captain.

"Wait! Please wait. I'm not a bill collector. I'm just trying to find some answers that may involve him."

Maureen grew curious. "What type of answers? Is this about the property over on Madison that they want to turn into a park for that Confederate general?"

"What? No. I don't know anything about a park. I'm trying to help out a friend who may have known your late husband."

"Well, I can tell you that Stumpy didn't have any friends! What is your friend's name?"

"Gunsie Hayes. Most folks called him Cuz. He grew up with another boy named Ira."

Maureen tilted her head and quickly asked, "Is there any reward money for any of this information if it helps you find these fellers?"

"No, there's no reward money. I'm just trying to piece together what happened back in the summer of 1882."

Maureen stated, "I don't know how I can help, but come into the parlor and tell me about it."

After settling down in the front room, the captain asked, "I'd like to ask how Mr. Vendig died."

"He died of cholera."

With much surprise, the captain retorted, "Cholera?"

"Yes, he died of cholera. Oh, but don't worry," she said while pointing towards the front yard. "We burned all of his things right out there in the front. I wanted to throw him in the fire too, but the doctor said something about some law preventing it or some such nonsense."

The captain made a couple of quick notes and then asked, "So a doctor was here and said he died of cholera?"

"Yes, Dr. Wesley Jarsdel was his name. Is there some problem I should know about? Why are you asking about my husband's death? I thought you were looking for those other men you mentioned."

After writing the doctor's name in his notes, he tried to explain his visit by first asking Maureen if she knew or had heard of Gunsie.

She replied, "That doesn't sound familiar to me, but that other boy's name, what was it, Ira? Well, let's just say you aren't the first person to be asking about him."

"Please explain!"

"Very well. You have to understand that my husband was a ruthless and secretive rapscallion. I felt compelled to snoop through his papers every chance I got to protect myself in the event he ever tried to pull some fast scheme on me. One day, I came across some papers about three children. At first, I thought they were my husband's children from a previous marriage, but they had a different last name. I didn't think much of it until a year or so later when I saw an advertisement in the personal section of the newspaper. Some woman was looking for her three lost children. What caught my eye was that the last name for the children was Vendig. The lady in the ad gave her last name as Gleason. I went back to the desk and dug out the paper I'd seen earlier and saw where the three children listed all had the last name of Gleason too."

Sitting up straight in his chair, he quickly asked what she did then.

"My first thought was that if this lady was spending money for an advertisement in the paper, she might be willing to offer a reward of some type for information. I sent her a letter asking how much the information was worth to her. Her name was Glenda. Anyway, she must've seen the return address on the post because about three weeks later, she showed up here asking what I knew. She looked desperate, and her clothes didn't seem to convey a feeling that she had money so I just told her to check out St. Peter's Orphanage. She thanked me and asked me not to tell my husband she'd come by."

"When was this?" the captain asked.

"Oh, it was maybe a week before my husband died."

"Did you ever tell your husband that she was in town?"

"No chance to. Only saw him a couple of times after I met her, and let's just say he wasn't in a talkative mood, either time."

Looking up from his note taking, the captain asked, "By any chance, do you still have those papers that had the orphans' names on it?"

Maureen sat forward and tersely replied, "You must be too busy writing in your ledger there to actually hear what I told you! As soon as he died, everything of his, including all his papers, was burned in a big fire out front."

Believing he had finally outstayed his welcome, he thanked Maureen for the information she'd given him and left.

While reading over his notes, the captain continued to think that Cuz's friend Ira had played some significant role in Stumpy's death. Perhaps Ira really was Stumpy's son, and he came back to kill the man who had abandoned him to an orphanage. However, the captain was disappointed to realize that Cuz still could have killed Stumpy on Ira's behalf. Either way, he needed to find out more about it. He quickly looked around to get his bearings and then darted off to St. Peters Orphanage.

After arriving at the orphanage, the captain eventually met Father O'Malley. He was an elderly gentleman with striking, avuncular features. The two men found it very easy to speak with one another as they went to the main office. The captain quickly explained his interest in finding out more about Gunsie's and Ira's pasts to better understand their actions later in life.

Father O'Malley retrieved a file and skimmed through it to refresh his memory before telling the captain the story about how Ira and his siblings came to be in his care.

"The orphaned Gleasons were a very sad story, indeed. There was this man, Clarence Green Vendig, who was married to a lady we later learned to be Glenda Gleason. Glenda had an illicit affair with a neighbor who fathered her three children. The three children were raised by Mr. Vendig as his own."

He continued, "Her oldest was a son, Ira. A couple of years later, Glenda gave birth to a daughter named Sara. The following year, Glenda's third child was born. His name was J.J. We never found out if J.J. actually had a more specific name. All three children were fathered by the neighbor, but were raised without Glenda's husband finding out."

Father O'Malley removed his glasses and placed them on the desk. He could tell the remaining part of the story from memory. "In 1868, Mr. Vendig found out the truth about the children he'd been raising. The embarrassment of the deception and infidelity led to a quick and ferocious divorce. The court granted Mr. Vendig's petition for custody of the bastard children since their mother was shown to be an adulterer and therefore unfit to be their mother."

"Shortly after the divorce was finalized, Mr. Vendig arrived here and abandoned the three children into our care. At the time, he claimed that the children's parents were both dead. We were only told their last name was Gleason."

The elderly man rubbed his eye as he glanced out the window. "Ira was five and couldn't grasp any of it. Nonetheless, he instinctively stepped in to try to care for his three-year-old sister and his two-year-old brother. While he was nurturing and caring for his siblings, he was not a doctor nor a miracle-worker. Sara came down with diphtheria and died in March of 1870."

"J.J. befriended another boy in the orphanage who was his age. It was the boy you mentioned earlier, Gunsie Hayes. Gunsie was sort of a part-time resident since his father took him out for a day or two each month. At least his father would come by to spend some time with him. In any event, J.J. died of yellow fever in 1873 at the age of seven. The following period of grief brought Ira and Gunsie closer together. Over the next couple of years, whenever Mr. Hayes took Gunsie out for the day, he started taking Ira too. Once Gunsie turned 10 and Ira was 13, Mr. Hayes took both boys out of the orphanage to live with him. He thought they were old enough to be left alone after school and that Ira was grounded well enough to deal with any problems that might arise."

The captain shook his head in disbelief. "What sort of person would take custody of children just to turn around and abandon them at an orphanage?"

Father O'Malley calmly replied, "The same sort of man who left the children with only the clothes on their backs while he took their remaining clothes to sell for his own profit."

Still in disbelief, the captain tried to focus on the more pertinent facts. "Just so that I clearly understand this, Clarence Green Vendig reared Ira and his siblings as his own. Then, after learning that he wasn't the father of any of the children, he brought them here to St. Peter's and abandoned them. Is this correct?"

Father O'Malley nodded his head and added that the Gleasons' story was by no means the saddest of the orphans that he had cared for over the years. With a raised eyebrow, he casually mentioned, "We're always looking for young couples who'd be willing to adopt."

As if he hadn't heard the previous comment, the captain quickly asked, "Did Mrs. Gleason come here looking for her children?"

"Yes, I met her. I think her name was Gladys or Gwendolyn...No, it was Glenda Gleason."

"Do you happen to remember when she was here?"

Father O'Malley tapped his fingers on the desk as if this would help him remember somehow. "It was late June, I believe, back in 1882. It could have been early July though."

Sitting forward in his seat, the captain asked, "Is there any chance that you might recall what she asked or what you told her?"

"She asked about her children. I had to tell her that two of them had died. Naturally, she was devastated to have finally tracked them down only to learn that only one had survived. I told her that Ira used to come back to say hello from time to time, but had stopped coming by after the yellow fever epidemic of '79. I told her that he might have moved away before the fever returned to the city. You see, at that time, I just didn't know if he had survived the epidemic or not."

Tilting his head slightly, the captain asked, "Did you ever see Ira after you spoke with his mother?"

"Yes. That was the strangest coincidence. I saw both Ira and Gunsie on the afternoon of the Independence Day Festival we were having. I told Ira that I had met his mother only a few days earlier. He was very eager to find her, but I couldn't help him since I had no clue where she was. That's the last time I ever saw either of the boys. I always figured that they ran off to the outlands somewhere."

Taking notes at a feverish pace, the captain looked up and said, "So, Ira's mom and Ira were both here the week or two before July 4, 1882. Do you know if they ever found each other?"

Father O'Malley slowly shook his head. Then with a slight smile, he said, "I would like to think they finally found each other."

After leaving the orphanage, the captain's curiosity was soaring, wondering if Ira and his mother ever met up or not. He quickly went over his notes to see if the widows had mentioned seeing Ira around that time. After not finding any such reference, he decided to just swing by and ask them about it on his way home. He was hoping their daily chores had been completed and that he wouldn't be wrangled into some type of menial task.

Approaching the house, he heard Miss Annie yelling at some man dragging a large branch across the yard "Watch what you're doing there! You're leaving broken branches all over the yard dragging like that!"

The captain, glad that it wasn't him getting yelled at, quietly snickered to himself as he stepped onto the front porch. "Good afternoon, ladies."

Miss Annie quietly nodded as Miss Jess giggled slightly as she boldly asked, "Hello, captain, did you bring us some of that delicious currant wine that your nice father-in-law makes?"

Before the captain could speak, Miss Annie blurted, "You don't see him carrying anything other than that notepad, do you?"

"I only have a couple more questions for you."

Miss Jess eagerly asked, "About Cuz?"

"Actually, no. It's about Ira."

The widows looked at the captain with a puzzled expression as he continued. "Did either of you see Ira around the time Cuz left town?"

Both ladies shook their heads. "The last time we saw Ira was about the time we took Cuz in to live with us."

"Did either of you ever hear from Ira's mother?"

The two ladies looked at each other as if they were trying to recall some distant memory. Miss Annie answered, "Yes, there was a lady who came by to visit us who claimed to be Ira's mother. How she figured out we knew him will always be a mystery. I can't think of what her name was."

The captain offered, "Was it Glenda Gleason?"

"Yes! That's what her name was."

Miss Jess added, "I seem to remember that she came by just a day or so before Cuz left. Isn't that right, Annie?"

Annie nodded as the captain asked if they knew whether or not Ira and his mother ever found each other.

The two ladies just shook their heads. "We didn't see or hear anything about Ira or his mother since her surprise visit."

Miss Annie yelled over to the man in the yard. "Don't put so much green stuff on that fire! What are you trying to do, smother it out?"

The captain smiled and thanked the widows for their help.

Miss Jess smiled and coyly replied, "A bottle of that currant wine would go a long way to letting us know how much you appreciated our helpfulness."

Miss Annie just folded her arms, smiled, and gave one notable nod of the head signaling her agreement.

Chapter Seven

Cause of Death

Once back at his mother-in-law's house, he fell into one of the parlor chairs. Polly served him a cold drink as he began to tell her about his day. Immediately, she stopped him. "My mother is fascinated about this investigation of yours and will want to know all about it. So, save your breath since you'll just have to repeat it all over again for her at dinner."

He laughed but was content to sit back and listen to Polly tell him about her day.

As promised, over dinner, Lavinia began to ask her son-in-law about his recent findings. He actually found it helpful to discuss it with someone. He began by telling them about the orphanage and how Stumpy abandoned the three children there. Both Lavinia and Polly were aghast at how callously Stumpy had rid himself of the responsibility for the children, not to mention the fact that he'd left the children with only the clothes that they were wearing.

The captain told the ladies about learning that Ira and his mother were both in town around the time Stumpy died. Lavinia remarked, "Well, both of them certainly had a reason to want Stumpy dead!"

"You didn't meet his widow! She clearly was pleased about him dying. She actually had a bonfire in their front yard to burn everything that reminded her of him right after he died!" he told them.

Polly tried to list the suspects with motives to kill Stumpy. "Your patient, Cuz, claims he killed Stumpy and that's why he left town. He didn't tell you why he killed him, but you believe it's because Stumpy killed his mother. Ira was abandoned at the orphanage by Stumpy and was led to believe that his real parents were dead. His two siblings died shortly afterwards. You know he was in town around the time Stumpy died and believe he could have killed him out of revenge. There is also the possibility that Ira's mother, who was seen in town near the same time, could have killed this wicked man for taking her children away from her only to leave them at an orphanage where two of them died. That's certainly a motive for murder."

Lavinia, without looking up, added, "I'd have killed him twice for that!"

"Don't forget his widow," the captain added.

Again, Lavinia contributed her opinion. "You certainly have to include her in your list of suspects. She despised him since day one! I'm telling you the truth!"

The captain nodded as he said, "After talking with her, I'd be very surprised to hear that she shed even a single tear over his death." He took a quick bite before adding, "Even if we add all of the people he swindled, which includes most of the prostitutes who were here then, and all of the homeowners he bamboozled, which includes the widows, even with this lengthy list of suspects, the fact remains that Cuz is the only one who has confessed to killing him."

The three sat quietly as they pondered the captain's observation. Polly looked at her husband and asked, "What was Stumpy's official cause of death?"

"According to Cuz, he hit Stumpy and he stumbled and fell to the floor, hitting his head on a table. According to his widow, Stumpy died of cholera." The captain nodded his head as he started to flash a grin of enlightenment, "If I can show Cuz the death certificate that indicates Stumpy died of cholera, then he would realize that he couldn't possibly have killed him."

With a sparkle in her eye, Lavinia asked the captain, "So, you appreciate our assistance in helping you with your little investigation, do you?"

"Well, of course I appreciate your valuable contributions."

"Good! Then you can do the dishes while Polly and I pick out an after-dinner wine."

As they all laughed and the captain accepted the assignment, he said, "Yes, I will happily do the dishes as a sign of my appreciation. I do have a question for you about the wine. Do you have any of the currant wine left? It was a big hit with the widows, and I would like to give them a bottle if possible."

Lavinia promised to see if they still had a bottle left.

Early Monday morning, the captain headed off to the police department and was happy to see Allen Vickery was on duty. "Good morning, Sarge. Did you have a nice Palm Sunday yesterday?"

With only a mildly suspicious expression, Sarge replied, "Good morning, captain. Yes, my family and I had a very nice day yesterday. Spring is certainly in the air. Now, what, may I ask, brings you in here so early this morning?"

Pulling out his notepad for reference, the captain said, "The last time I was in here you mentioned that Clarence Green Vendig disappeared around 1882. Well, I came across information that he died on, or shortly after, July 4, 1882. I was wondering if you could look in your records to see if there's any mention of it."

Still displaying an expression of mild suspicion, Sarge reach for the appropriate log and began flipping pages. He carefully reviewed every entry for three days before and after the specific date the captain had mentioned. He found no records for Stumpy's death.

The captain thanked Sarge for checking for him. He then stated that he was glad there was no record since it would indicate that Stumpy had not been murdered. Sarge just snickered as he replied, "What it means is that no one filed a complaint on his behalf. If he was such a villainous man and everyone wanted him dead, who would have bothered telling us about it?"

"I see your point," the captain replied before asking, "Where are the death certificates kept?"

Closing the log book, Sarge said, "You'll need to go over to the Board of Health for that. They are located at 154 Front Street. Only you won't find individual certificates. They maintain a ledger book similar to these precinct logs. That's how they record the deaths in the city, providing they are reported to them."

Right as Sarge was about to ask why the captain was interested in a 17-year-old death, the captain said, "Thank you, Sarge. I really appreciate the information. Enjoy your cornbread—it smells incredibly delicious!"

Sarge just thanked him for the compliment and thought that he might get a straight answer from the captain the next time he saw him.

The clerk at the Board of Health was a very friendly elderly lady who enjoyed answering questions about the department's records. As soon as the captain furnished her with a name and date, she happily began searching for the information. She made random small talk as she researched the records; commenting on the spring flowers blooming in front of her home and the distant steamboat whistle they could hear.

She finally found the entry in the ledger. "Here it is. Clarence Green Vendig...That's interesting. It has the word Stumpy in quotation marks next to his name."

The captain mentioned that Stumpy was Mr. Vendig's nickname.

"Oh, I see. Well, it says here that Mr. Vendig died of cholera on July 5, 1882." Then, with a slight sneer, she added, "It says that Doctor Wesley Jarsdel was present in the home at the time of death."

Noticing her obvious reaction to the doctor's name, the captain asked, "Do you know Doctor Jarsdel?"

Forcing her best customer service demeanor in a weak attempt to mask her true feelings, she replied, "Well, this doctor also has a nickname. It's Fishhook. That should tell you right there that he spends more time fishing than with his patients." Then, under her breath, she mumbled, "Fishing and drinking, that is."

The captain asked a few more questions and learned that the doctor was still in practice and where his office was located. He thanked the clerk for her time and information.

Thinking that one last confirmation from the doctor who had signed the death certificate would be sufficient to convince Cuz that he had not killed Stumpy, the captain headed towards the doctor's office. Not surprisingly, the office was only a few blocks from Stumpy's house. Just a block before arriving at Doctor Jarsdel's office, the captain noticed a neighborhood apothecary.

He stopped for a moment in front of the store and thought that the chances were high that Stumpy may have been prescribed medicine from this drugstore. Especially since Doctor Jarsdel's office was a block away and Stumpy's house was only three blocks away, the druggist might have additional records to prove Stumpy died of cholera. The captain was gaining hope that he could get enough evidence to convince Cuz of his innocence.

Upon entering the store, he was instantly greeted by a man with a thick Italian accent asking how he could be of service. The captain introduced himself as a military doctor researching some old records. He then asked if the pharmacist could find records of medicines prescribed back in the summer of 1882.

"Hello, I am Giovanni Liguori. You can call me Vanni. This is my business, and I have very good records. My files are arranged by name. Do you have a name that would be on the record?"

The captain stuttered a little bit as he fumbled with his notepad. There was something about the name Liguori that was haunting him. Once he flipped to the notes from his discussion with Stumpy's widow, he found it. She was now married to a Liguori.

"So, tell me, Vanni, is your wife's name Maureen?"

Vanni made a repulsed face and pretended to spit on the floor as he exclaimed, "Zoccola!" After composing himself slightly, he continued, "My brother Tony, he married that woman. She is, how you say, jezebel. You understand?"

Nodding his head, he asked, "When did Tony and Maureen get married?"

Vanni shook his head as he mumbled something in Italian. Noticing the captain's confused expression, he slowed down and said, "Her first husband was not even cold in the ground, and they were getting married. Our mamma would have had a broken heart to see who her beloved Tony married.”

The two men quietly shook their heads for a few seconds at the situation before the captain explained his question. “Maureen's late husband, did he receive any camphor from here? He may have been prescribed it for cholera around July first through July fourth, 1882.”

Vanni smiled and again boasted about his excellent records. He seemed very pleased to talk about something other than his sister-in-law. After a few minutes thumbing through his records, he said, “I'm not finding whether he got any camphor from here.” Then, with a slight tilt of the head, he added, “This is strange. We have records of several deliveries of arsenic. Looks like they had a big rat problem.”

The captain realized that the symptoms from arsenic poisoning and cholera are very similar. Was Stumpy poisoned, or did he actually die of cholera? He briefly thought that it didn't matter, since either way it seemed Stumpy's death didn't come from a shove and a fall.

The captain's face grew stern as he realized that he had to know what had actually happened, not only for his own peace of mind, but also to be able to convince Cuz that he wasn't responsible for the death.

Vanni was thanked for his help and information. As the captain turned to leave, Vanni pleaded, “Please, captain, my business is small. Won't you please buy something? Maybe some rock candy?”

Noticing some small cards with a picture of the Gayosc Hotel on them, he asked, “Are these those new private mailing cards I've heard about?”

Vanni turned on the sales pitch and explained, "The post office, they lose-a their monopoly on the postcard market, you know? Now I sell these picture cards. We just not can call 'em postcards."

The captain purchased five and then went on his way.

As soon as he turned the corner, he witnessed an argument between two men on a doorstep. As he neared the confrontation, he could hear the man who was starting to walk away from the door yelling, "...You drunk old fool! You probably couldn't even bandage a dead man!"

The man in the doorway just waved off his verbal attacker, and then turned and walked back inside. Walking past the irate patient, the captain tried to hear what he was mumbling about, but could not make sense of it. His suspicions that the man in the doorway was Dr. Jarsdel were soon proved to be true as he arrived at the designated address.

Walking into the empty office, he spotted the doctor through a partially open doorway leading to an examination room. Knocking on the door before entering, the captain saw the doctor quickly trying to hide a flask from which he had just taken a sizable swig.

Annoyed, the doctor demanded, "Why'd you come in my office like this?"

"Please forgive the unannounced visit. There was no one at the clerk's desk. I'm Captain Hodge from..."

"Good for you! Am I supposed to salute or something?" Doctor Jarsdel interrupted. Then, realizing the captain was not a patient, he walked over to a cabinet retrieving a bottle of bourbon before he said, "State your business—I ain't got all day to listen to folk wandering in off the street. I'm very busy here!"

Mustering his best commanding tone, the captain barked, "I am a military doctor investigating the death of one of your patients. His name was..."

Again interrupting the captain, Doctor Jarsdel asked, "Yankee or Rebel? I treated both. If it was a Yankee, I made sure to make bullet extraction especially painful. Funny how I never had anything for the pain when I was working on Yankee patients."

The captain firmly stood his ground and stated, "To the best of my knowledge, Clarence Green Vendig never served in the military."

"Clarence who? What makes you think I was this man's doctor?"

The captain answered, "You signed his death certificate. You may have known him by his nickname—Stumpy."

"Oh, Stumpy! Yes, I knew the miserable cheat. You are correct—he is dead."

"You signed the death certificate saying that he died of cholera."

The old drunk doctor began re-filling his flask as he said, "Cholera? Is that what finally got ole Stumpy?"

Pushing for some type of legitimate answer, the captain said, "That's what you said the cause of death was on the death certificate. Was it cholera or not?"

Returning the remaining bourbon to the cabinet, Doctor Jarsdel snipped, "If that's what I put on the ledger, then that's what he died of. Now close the door on your way out."

"Listen, I just need to know how you determined his death was due to cholera rather than a blow to his head or arsenic poisoning. Do you even remember seeing him before you signed off on his cause of death?"

After licking the outside of his flask where he had spilled a little bourbon, Doctor Jarsdel gave the captain a look that clearly showed that he didn't appreciate being questioned. "Yes, I looked at him. I got close enough to make sure he was dead. Then I got just a tad closer so I could tell him that while he always cheated everyone else, he couldn't cheat death."

Relentlessly, the captain asked, "Had you diagnosed cholera before his death? Did you see him die?"

"He was still warm when I got there, as I remember, so he hadn't been dead long. However, it had been long enough for his widow and that Italian fellow to start a bonfire in the front yard and start burning his clothes."

"You didn't treat him for cholera before his death?"

Placing the flask in his jacket pocket, the doctor confirmed that he had not been treating Stumpy before his death.

With frustration mounting in his tone, the captain again asked, "Then why did you conclude it was cholera?"

Raising his voice, the doctor replied, "I asked about his symptoms and was told that he had diarrhea, vomiting, confusion, and seizures, and then he went into a coma for a bit before he finally died. That's what happens to people with cholera. It's not that uncommon around these parts."

Tersely, the captain pointed out that those same symptoms could be caused by arsenic poisoning.

The doctor defiantly replied, "I probably had five other cases of cholera in the four weeks before Stumpy died. Are you saying all those others died of arsenic too? Besides, you don't burn the clothes of arsenic victims!"

The captain, fighting to maintain his composure, said, "If I understand the events clearly, you were called after Stumpy died and based your determination that he died of cholera on the fact that they were already burning his clothes. Is this correct?"

Doctor Jarsdel put his hands on his hips and blatantly said, "At this point, what damn difference does it make? The world is better off without him! I tell you this—if he was poisoned and my death certificate helped a killer get away with it, well if word got out about that, I'd never have to buy a drink in this town ever again!"

Realizing that nothing good could come from continuing to discuss the matter, the captain promptly left the office. His mind was racing with what his next steps should be. Should he just stop now and convince Cuz that Stumpy died of a disease and not from anything Cuz had done? Should he keep trying to get evidence as to how Stumpy died? What should he do? More importantly, what could he do and be at peace with himself afterwards?

When he noticed where he was, he knew what he had to do. He marched into the police precinct and explained the whole story to Sarge. When he was done, Sarge looked at him and simply asked, "What does any of this have to do with me?"

Without saying a word, the captain's expression seemed to ask Sarge if he seriously wanted to allow a potential murder go uninvestigated.

Reactively, Sarge said, "I don't know how things are where you come from, but here in Memphis, when somebody bad dies—we're all right with that. We move on and forget about it. We certainly don't wait 17 years and stir everything back up again!"

"Look, Sarge," the captain pleaded, "I have a soldier who claims he killed Stumpy by shoving him into some furniture. If we do a proper autopsy, we'll know immediately if Stumpy died from a head wound. If he did, well then, you'll have your killer."

"What if there ain't no head wound?" Sarge asked stubbornly.

The captain just shrugged his shoulders and said, "If that's the case, we'll know he died of something else."

Sarge just looked at the captain blankly for a moment. He then reached down into his open desk drawer and pulled out a small basket filled with hush puppies. Taking one for himself, he offered them to the captain, as he said, "Maybe Judge Selby will give you authority to dig Stumpy up and review the autopsy records. Don't let the title fool you, he don't know much about the law and has never passed that there bar examination lawyers are supposed to have, but he got elected to the job anyway. Yes, sir, he might just be your man."

Biting into the hush puppy, the captain's eyes widened as he savored the treat. "This is the spiciest hush puppy I think I've ever had!"

"Jalapeño peppers—that's what gives it a little kick, don't you think? Yes, sir! This ain't your momma's hush puppies!"

Grabbing his hat, Sarge told the captain he'd take him to the judge's office and introduce him. On the walk over, Sarge said, "You know, ever since you've been poking around with this case, I really thought you'd learn that Eli and his buddies had something to do with Stumpy's death."

Puzzled, the captain asked for clarification. "Why would you think the editor of the newspaper would be involved in anyone's death?"

Sarge calmly replied, "I thought you knew. Eli and his vigilante Klan friends would deal out their own brand of justice when they thought proper legal channels weren't fixing the problem. If you know what I mean. I just thought Eli found out about Stumpy and, well, let's just say that they would've taken care of it."

Before the captain could respond, they had arrived at the judge's office. They caught Judge Selby as he was leaving for the tavern. Sarge, under his breath, told the captain that they got there at the perfect time.

Immediately, Sarge started spouting off all types of random facts and figures about crime in the city and how it would be terrible to let crime go unpunished. Every now and then, he would ask the judge random questions about his family or the new horse he had recently purchased. He then slid a document in front of the judge and suggested that all he needed to do was sign where indicated and that they would then be on their way.

The judge quickly looked at his pocket watch and would do almost anything to get to the tavern for a drink. He quickly signed the form and asked that future visits occur earlier in the day.

As Judge Selby stormed off, the captain looked at Sarge and exclaimed, "You are a real shyster, do you know that? The judge didn't even look at the form."

Sarge smiled and handed the form to the captain as he said, "That's Judge Selby for you. He never reads anything. A few years ago, a bank got him to sign his own eviction notice! Anyway, here's your authorization to dig up Stumpy. I hope you find what you're looking for."

The captain filed the document with the coroner's office and was told that he should return the following day for some type of status report on the request.

With Sarge's comments about Eli and the vigilantes still buzzing around his head, the captain began to wonder if he had been steered away from pertinent information concerning his investigation. Wanting to get an immediate answer, he went straight to the newspaper to confront Eli personally.

As soon as he spotted Eli in his office, the captain decided to take a calm approach with him. "Eli! How are you doing? Have you or J.B. found anything new about the case?"

Eli was happy to see the captain and began laying out several facts that they had uncovered.

The captain stopped him and said, "Before we get into all of this, I need to ask you something." Eli took his glasses off and waited for the captain's question. "Did you use to ride with vigilantes in these parts?"

Eli's head drooped slightly as he said, "I never rode with them—not once. Years ago, when Yankees decided what was right or wrong, they frequently took the opportunity to pervert the course of justice on behalf of their northern friends. When I saw or heard of such transgressions, well, I passed the information along to some associates who facilitated a far more equitable form of justice."

Eli could see that the captain was having difficulty understanding what the vigilantes were doing. "Three different women working over at the gas works were found after being raped and murdered. Co-workers and some locals identified a man as the one responsible. The union-controlled court said there was insufficient evidence to prosecute him. A few days later, the killer was found swinging from a tree by a noose. No other women from the gas works became victims. Two men were found behind a saloon after being stabbed to death. Several customers in the bar admitted seeing the stabbings and pointed out the man responsible. Because this killer was a councilman's brother, the union officers claimed the witnesses had been drinking and were unreliable. I hear they never did find his body, but I can tell you no one else has turned up stabbed like those first two fellows."

Shaking his head slowly, the captain asked, "Did you have anything to do with Stumpy's death?"

Eli tilted his head and confidently stated, "I haven't had anything to do with vigilante justice since Hayes became president in 1877!" Again seeing the captain's confusion, he elaborated, "The deal that was made to give Rutherford B. Hayes the White House even though he didn't win the election resulted in the end of Reconstruction. We were able to man our own courts and even our own prosecutor's offices. The need for vigilantes vanished when we could pursue legitimate justice."

Looking Eli directly in the eye, the captain asked, "So you played no part in Stumpy's death?"

"No. To be honest, though, if I'd known about Stumpy killing Austina, I probably would've passed his name along to my associates. If that had been the case, he would have been dealt with 14 years earlier than he was. Now, can I show you what J.B. found in the archives?"

After a nod and a couple of understanding smiles, the two men started reviewing the most recent findings. For the most part, the articles confirmed information the captain had collected so far in his various meetings. The captain then shared his recent findings with Eli and the fact that he would be meeting with the coroner on the following day to see if they could determine Stumpy's true cause of death.

Realizing the hour, the captain invited Eli to join him for dinner at his mother-in-law's house. Eli got wide-eyed as he stood and said, "My dear friend, I rarely turn down an invitation for a good home-cooked meal. I suggest we leave at once. Don't you agree?"

The captain laughed as he nodded and then began to lead the way.

At one point along their way, Eli stopped to look down towards the Mississippi river and across to the sun setting over Arkansas. The captain had continued on for several feet before he realized Eli had stopped.

Before the captain could ask if anything was wrong, Eli pointed to the river bridge and firmly stated, "That bridge is only a few years old, and it has already benefited this old river town. Mark my words—this city is destined for greatness! We are poised on the edge of westward expansion. States are popping up throughout the outlands: Utah, Montana, the Dakotas. I bet even the Indian Territories will become a state in a few years. Those new states need people and supplies, and thanks to that bridge, Memphis can supply them with all their needs."

The captain agreed, adding, "The Yukon gold rush is just the latest of what will inevitably be other large discoveries of gold, silver, and gemstones throughout the Rocky Mountains. More important is the fact that a growing nation needs more farmland. The plains will help feed the growing populations back East. There's a lot of exciting new things happening all across the West from Texas to Washington and from California to North Dakota. So, tell me, Eli, why didn't you go westward and start a newspaper reporting on the new frontier?"

Eli scoffed before giving a serious response. "The lure of the outlands is mighty powerful. Cuz and Ira felt the powerful magnetism that compelled them to explore parts unknown. Yes, the attraction to go west is hard to fight. It might be easier to stop the river from flowing..." Eli stopped for a moment before continuing, "I've written my

story. The west is for people who have several more chap-
ters to write before they are done."

Again, there was a moment of contemplative silence before
Eli blurted, "You mentioned something about a good
home-cooked meal, didn't you?"

Chapter Eight

Taking Credit

Once they arrived, the captain introduced Eli to Polly and Lavinia, and asked if it would be all right for him to join them for dinner. Of course the ladies agreed, even though Lavinia appeared slightly annoyed about the short notice. After all, who brings company to dinner on a Monday night?

Polly, sensing her mother's bewilderment over the late-arriving guest, started to speak to her when Lavinia said, "It'll be fine. It isn't a problem at all. We're having stew and potatoes. We can easily set another place at the table."

Polly just looked at her mother as if she was seeking some type of assurance that she was really at peace with the situation. Lavinia added, "Come to think of it, I believe I'm actually happy that he's comfortable enough to ask his acquaintances to dinner here if he wants."

Polly and her mother finished setting the table as Eli layered on a multitude of compliments about the wonderful mouth-watering smells and the attractiveness of the setting. The captain assisted Polly with her chair, as Eli promptly did the same for Lavinia.

Just as the captain started to reach for the ladle to serve the ladies, there was a knock at the front door. The captain quickly said, "I'll see who it is. Please start without me."

Answering the door, he was surprised to see Miss Jess on the doorstep. Shocked at her unexpected visit, he politely asked her why she was there.

"I killed him!" she exclaimed defiantly. "Is this when you arrest me and haul me to prison?"

She saw his baffled expression of disbelief. "Do you hear me, young man? I'm responsible for killing Stumpy!" She then smiled slightly as she leaned towards the captain and added, "You know, he really hated it when people called him that."

After finally recovering from his initial shock, he asked her to step into the parlor and explain herself. She instantly started talking about how evil and cruel Stumpy was and that he was always taking advantage of everyone he met. "In fact," she continued, "my husband was on his deathbed when Stumpy weaseled his way in and convinced him to sign a bunch of papers. The next thing I knew, my husband had died and Stumpy was evicting me, claiming the home now belonged to him."

Her back was towards the dining room so Miss Jess couldn't see Eli, Polly, and Lavinia standing quietly in the doorway eavesdropping on her confession. The captain was trying not to be distracted by their presence, but couldn't avoid seeing Eli making wild gestures and mouthing something. Eli was apparently suggesting he should ask Miss Jess how she killed Stumpy.

"Miss Jess, this all occurred such a long time ago. Are you sure that you killed him?" he asked.

"Oh, I'm very sure. I'm not proud of it, but I'm responsible nonetheless. Are you a religious man?"

The captain squirmed a little in his chair as he answered, "Well, uh, yes. I try to be."

Miss Jess continued, "Well, it's true what the preacher says—prayer is a powerful thing—very powerful. I hated that man in a way I had never before hated another human being. I prayed for him to die, and then the next thing I knew—he was dead. So you see, I'm responsible for his death."

The captain couldn't help noticing Eli trying to refrain from laughing as Polly and her mother just looked on in disbelief. He then asked Miss Jess for clarification. "Just for my records, you prayed for his death and this is what caused him to die. Is this correct?"

With wide-eyed conviction, Miss Jess nodded as she responded, "Never underestimate the power of prayer."

Lost for a response, he stood and decided to introduce her to the other three who were entering the parlor to greet her. As Lavinia was inviting her to join them for dinner, there was another knock on the door. This time, however, they could hear a voice. It was Miss Annie shouting, "Jess? Jess, are you in there? Captain Hodge, is Jess in there with you?"

Miss Jess seemed to indicate she didn't want Miss Annie to know that she had come there to confess. Honoring her wishes, the three escorted her into the dining room while the captain answered the door.

"Miss Annie, what a surprise. What brings you here?"

Just as she was about to respond, the captain seized the opportunity to interrupt her as she had done to him on previous occasions. "Wait! Don't tell me. You came to get a bottle of that currant wine you ladies are so fond of, correct?" He then motioned for her to come inside.

As she stepped through the door, she quickly looked around for Jess. Again, as she started to speak, the captain playfully interrupted. "My wife, mother-in-law, and I were just sitting down to dinner; would you like to join us?"

Finally seizing control of the conversation, Miss Annie blurted, "Jess is on her way over here to confess to you that she killed Stumpy."

Displaying his best look of surprise, he simply gasped slightly as he said, "No! Really?"

Miss Annie continued, "Yes, gol darn it! She left me a note telling me all about it. She said she'll probably be sent to some prison up north somewhere and wanted me to send her some of her favorite turnip greens when they're picked later in the summer. If'n she ain't hung by then. Listen here, captain, she ain't never killed nobody!"

"You seem awful sure of that," he interjected.

"Just as sure as I am that it weren't Cuz dat killed him neither!" she added.

As the captain took a breath to start to ask how she could be so sure, Miss Annie continued, "Look here, I went looking for Cuz that night. Someone told me they thought they saw him over on South Lauderdale, so I went over there When I turned the corner, I heard a bunch of fireworks at the same time that I saw a woman in the street pointing a gun towards an open window. I couldn't tell if she actually fired the gun or was just pointing it. After she ran off, I noticed that the house she was pointing at was Stumpy's So, you see? It couldn't have been anyone other than that woman who done killed Stumpy."

"Did you see the woman's face?"

"No, but I remember thinking she looked a lot like that gal who came around claiming to be Ira's mom."

The captain quickly asked, "All these years afterwards, you can't be sure if a gun was actually fired through the open window nor can you be certain as to the identity of the female shooter. Is this what you are telling me?"

Miss Annie nodded as she said, "I just kept looking for Cuz and kept my nose out of other people's business."

Standing up, he asked her to follow him into the dining room. Once they entered, the captain got everyone's attention and then emphatically stated: "Listen to me, both of you. Miss Jess, you didn't kill Stumpy with your prayers! Miss Annie, you did not see Stumpy being shot! Based on the information I have from his widow and the attending physician at the time of his death, Stumpy died of cholera. If he had had a bullet wound in him, I would think that even Doctor Jarsdel would have noticed it."

Lavinia stood up and asked Miss Annie, "Won't you join us for dinner? I'm sure there is plenty."

Miss Annie started to decline, but noticed Miss Jess already seated next to Eli. She quickly accepted the invitation. As the captain was motioning her to a chair across from Miss Jess, Miss Annie marched around the table to take the available seat on the other side of Eli. Eli seemed to enjoy the two widows' attention.

As dinner progressed, Lavinia asked, "Daniel, if Mr. Vendig died of cholera, does this mean your investigation is over, and you'll be able to convince your patient that he didn't murder him?"

Everyone seemed to stop in their tracks to hear the captain's response. "I hope Cuz will believe me and agree to accept the award he has earned. I hope when I meet with the coroner and get the final autopsy results, we'll be able to determine the actual cause of death allowing us to close the book on this investigation."

Miss Annie barked, "Autopsy? You mean to say you dug up Stumpy to give him an autopsy?"

Miss Jess giggled as she leaned towards Polly as she whispered, "He really didn't like that nickname, you know?"

Eli interjected, "If we want to know the truth, we've got to do it. We hope we can give this Cuz fellow some peace of mind by proving that he isn't responsible for this man's death. At the same time, if we find out someone else was responsible, well, then we'll know who to thank for their services."

Miss Jess offered to serve Eli more stew as she smiled and told him, "You are such a wise man." She then gave him a sly little wink of affection. Eli accepted the flirtation gracefully while Miss Annie simply rolled her eyes in disbelief at the forwardness on display.

Lavinia, smiling slightly at the flirtation going on across the table, said, "Are you saying that you don't believe he died of cholera?"

The captain took his napkin and wiped his mouth before answering. "At this point, I'm anxiously awaiting the autopsy results to help me understand what actually happened. Cuz believes he killed Stumpy by shoving him so hard that he fell and hit his head. Cuz has real guilt over this action. He's fought in various battles trying to redeem himself for his wickedness. Cuz truly believes that he murdered Stumpy. What was his motive? He killed out of revenge for Stumpy's killing his mother. Then, more recently, Stumpy kicked him and his father out of their homes during the yellow fever epidemic."

Looking around the table, the captain continued. "Then we have Ira. Father O'Malley claims that Ira was here in town around the time Stumpy died. I haven't found anyone who witnessed Ira meeting his father, but did he? Did Ira meet his father and then murder him out of revenge for abandoning him at the orphanage with his siblings? If so, how did he kill him?"

"Speaking of Ira," the captain paused and looked at Miss Annie as he pointed to her, "We have a witness who claims to have seen Ira's mother pointing a gun at Stumpy's house. According to this witness, we can't be sure if anyone was actually wounded in the process or if the gun was even fired."

Tilting his head slightly as he continued, the captain said, "Next, we have Maureen Vendig, the non-grieving widow who seems to have had an enormous vermin problem prior to Stumpy's death. She loathed her husband for a number of reasons. Maureen wanted to be free of him, so she could marry Tony Liguori, the pharmacist's brother. Did she poison Stumpy? Is that what killed him?"

He then mentioned Miss Lolla as the next potential suspect, causing Miss Jess to say, "Awe, Miss Lolla was a very nice madam for her girls. She took real good care of them and was a very nice neighbor for us, wasn't she, Annie?"

Annie nodded and said, "Yes, she was a fine neighbor. She kept things quiet."

Smiling at the endorsement, the captain continued, "According to Miss Cairy, she thought Miss Lolla stabbed Stumpy out of revenge for terrorizing her girls, evicting her from her home, and then later, essentially running her out of business."

Again leaning towards Polly, Miss Jess said, "Cairy was always such a sweet girl. I think she was smitten with Cuz, you know?"

Sitting straight up in her chair with her hands on her hips, Miss Annie told the captain, "Miss Lolla would do almost anything to protect her girls."

In conclusion, the captain said, "Even with all of these theories and opinions as to how he died, the official cause of death was recorded as cholera. I hasten to point out that the doctor who certified the cause of death is a drunk who based his decision primarily on the information given to him by the widow rather than by any valid medical examination of the body at the time of death."

Eli summed up the story by saying, "In other words, we've been told that Stumpy died from a cracked skull, from being poisoned, from being shot, from being stabbed, and from disease. We certainly hope the autopsy will clear up the mystery for us."

Polly told her mother how much she enjoyed the meal. This resulted in the others following suit with a parade of compliments for the stew.

Lavinia blushed as she offered an after-dinner drink for anyone interested.

Both of the widows eagerly answered a resounding "Yes!"

Miss Jess, recognizing the fairly unladylike manner in which they responded, added, "I mean, yes, if it's not too much of a burden. Perhaps some wine maybe?"

Lavinia smiled as she went to see what she could find in the cellar. The widows continued to dote on Eli while the captain and Polly cleared the table.

Shortly, Lavinia returned with a bottle of wine and six glasses. "I found a bottle of cherry wine I think you will all enjoy."

Polly was the only one who seemed to think the wine was a bit too strong. The captain was acquiring a taste for it, while the older folks were savoring each sip to the fullest.

Eli was the first to announce his departure as he again lavished Lavinia with compliments on the meal as well as the after-dinner drinks. The widows wanted to walk with Eli so they hurried to express their appreciation as well. Lavinia stopped them only long enough to present them with a bottle of currant wine for them to take home with them. "My son-in-law told me how much you enjoyed this particular wine."

After the widows thanked her for the wine, Miss Annie walked over to the captain and firmly shook his hand as she said, "You're a good man, Captain Hodge. Thank you."

Miss Jess scurried over to the captain and before he realized it, she was giving him a big hug. "Oh thank you—thank you—thank you! You are so sweet to remember us."

Lavinia was smiling with pride that her husband's wine made the women so happy. The captain and Polly just chuckled lightly at the giddiness the widows showed over their gift.

Before stepping out of the door, Miss Jess turned and happily announced that she would pray for all of their good health. Given the power she claimed her prayers had, they were all very happy to stay on her good side.

The next day, when the captain arrived at the coroner's office, Doctor Chamberline greeted him professionally and took him to the examination room. Laid out on the over-sized table were some badly decomposed skeletal remains in a pile of dirt and clay. The coroner looked at the captain and said, "This is all we could find of Clarence Green Verdig. It appears he was simply shoved into a used burlap bag and buried without a casket in the pauper's section of Elmwood Cemetery."

Shaking his head in disbelief, the captain stated, "His widow must've really hated him since she didn't even want to incur the expense of a cheap pine box to bury him in."

Doctor Chamberline nodded and replied, "I wish I could say it surprised me. As a coroner, I see all types of behavior."

Focusing on the purpose of the exhumation, the captain asked if he'd learned anything from examining the remains.

The coroner smiled and remarked, "What I learned was that this man was not well liked! First, there are multiple skull fractures."

"Is that what killed him?" the captain impatiently asked.

Holding his hand up as if to request a moment more to explain, the coroner continued, "No. Two of the fractures seem to have healed, indicating they occurred a significant amount of time before his death. One fracture showed no signs of healing, so it may have been caused at, or near, his time of death. In my opinion, he did not die from this head wound."

The captain smiled since this was the primary answer he needed. Cuz did not murder Stumpy. Wanting to satisfy his remaining curiosity, he encouraged the coroner to continue explaining his findings.

"There's a chunk missing from his left humerus. It appears he may also have been shot at some point near his time of death. I doubt it killed him. Then there are several bone scars that possibly could indicate various knife attacks. The scars on his ribs, fingers, and shoulder were inflicted at various times before his death. From the looks of it, I can tell you that this man was in his share of back-alley fights."

With determination, the captain asked, "What about poisoning? Could the cause of death have been arsenic poisoning?"

The coroner pointed to a couple of the bones and said, "Yes, there are signs of arsenic in the remains."

"So, he did not die from cholera!" the captain exclaimed.

With a slight tilt of the head, the coroner corrected him. "I didn't say that. I can see the presence of arsenic in the bones but these remains are too decomposed for me to determine if the concentration was high enough to have killed him. In addition, cholera can only be found in the soft tissue. As you can see, there is none of that left to test."

The captain looked at the remains as he realized the coroner was correct. Even though he'd found arsenic in the remains, he couldn't definitively state that it had caused Stumpy's death. Furthermore, he couldn't prove that Stumpy had died of cholera, either.

For a moment, the captain grew upset, thinking that a murderer would go free and that Doctor Jarsdel would not be exposed as a drunken fool for overlooking the true cause of death. However, he realized that his mission for coming back to Memphis was now over. He had found the evidence he needed to convince Cuz that he had not murdered Stumpy.

Dr. Chamberline broke the silence. "If there is nothing else you need to know, I'll have Mr. Vendig sent back to Elmwood to be re-interred."

Both men looked at the pile of dirt and bones, and thought of how undignified Stumpy's burial had been. The coroner reflectively said, "It seems a shame to bury him again without so much as a cheap wooden box."

Smiling slightly, the captain looked at the coroner and replied, "Doctor, from everyone I've talked to regarding this man, it's probably the most fitting burial he could have. The fact that it will now happen to him twice will be a great comfort to many."

Chapter Nine

The Honor

Now that the captain's mission had concluded and he could confidently convince Cuz that he was not a murderer, he had only one remaining obligation in Memphis before returning to his post. He had promised his wife and mother-in-law that they would attend Easter service. It was probably for the best since this would delay their departure until Monday morning, at the earliest. This would allow the captain time to contact a couple of people who had helped him with his investigation.

On Friday, the captain noticed a teenager doing yardwork a couple doors away. He walked over and asked the young man if he was interested in making some money doing chores and running errands. The lad eagerly agreed, but the captain asked him to wait for the location. He then handed the boy an address written on a piece of paper and asked if he could be there in an hour. After careful consideration, the boy smiled and said that he'd be there. The captain shook his hand and announced that they had a deal.

Returning to the house only long enough to hitch up the carriage and get Polly, the captain set out for the widows' house. He was happy to see that he had arrived before his hired hand. Polly commented, "I really like this area along Parkway. It's so fresh and beautiful out here. Maybe when you get out of the service, we can move out here. How would you feel about that?"

The captain quickly replied, "As long as we're at least four to six blocks away from the widows."

Polly laughed, knowing her husband was afraid they would have him busy doing chores all the time. Before she could speak, the widows came onto the porch arguing with one another. "It is the darkening of the moon that makes this the best time to plant!" Miss Jess stated emphatically.

Miss Annie propped her hands on her hips and fired back, "You plant crops and things you want to grow during a waxing moon! Not now—this is a waning moon."

With a stubborn, yet polite, determination, Miss Jess began to respond when she noticed their visitors approaching. "Lookie here, Annie—we gots visitors!"

Turning to see their guests walking up towards the house, Miss Annie called out, "Captain Hodge, would you tell this fool woman this ain't the time to be plant'n in the garden? Or don't they teach you fellows this stuff in army medical school?"

The captain mumbled to Polly, "On second thought, make that eight blocks away." As she fought back her laugh, the captain responded, "Well, no. The army didn't teach us about such things. However, I grew up on a farm, and my grandparents were very successful farmers. What they always taught me is that you don't plant crops during the last quarter of a waning moon."

Miss Annie victoriously crossed her arms and nodded her head in appreciation of the captain's validation of her side of the argument. The captain added, "The last quarter of the waning moon doesn't start until Monday, so actually you can plant certain crops today."

Now it was Miss Jess' turn to look smug in victory. Miss Annie quickly asked, "What crops did your grandfather suggest you plant at this point?"

"As I remember, he would only plant root crops after the full moon. Things like carrots, beets, onions, and potatoes. All the other crops he'd wait till after the new moon to plant."

Polly, sensing that her husband had annoyed both widows at this point, decided to change the subject. "We just stopped by to say goodbye."

Miss Jess quickly offered to serve tea, but they declined. As if on cue, the young man the captain had hired walked up.

The captain announced, "As a parting gift, I have hired this young man..." Realizing he didn't know his name, he asked, "I'm sorry, what was your name?"

The teenager stood up straight as he replied, "My name is Jeremy, sir."

After a quick nod, the captain looked back at the widows. "I have hired Jeremy here for a day's work. He can help with your yard, flowerbeds, garden, or boxes, if you wish. If you like his work, maybe you can hire him back from time to time in the future."

Miss Annie asked, "So, he's on the clock, is he?"

The captain and Jeremy both nodded.

Miss Annie fired back, "Well, let's get a move on! You ain't get'n paid to stand around look'n pretty!"

Miss Jess giggled as she softly said, "He is a handsome young man."

As Jeremy was being shown a list of chores, Miss Jess thanked the captain and Polly for their generosity. As they exchanged their farewells, Miss Jess asked the captain, "Please tell Cuz we miss him and that we would both love to see him again."

"I'll pass along your message."

Later in the afternoon back at Lavinia's house, the captain received a telegram. It read:

> "TO: Captain Daniel Hodge.
> Sergeant Gunsie Hayes to receive Certificate of Merit for his actions in Cuba. You are to return to duties on April 10, 1899, at latest.
> Colonel Dean"

He sighed disappointedly after reading the note. Polly had walked up and read it for herself.

"So it all worked out. This is what you wanted for him, isn't it?" she asked as she tried to understand his defeated expression.

He forced a smile as he looked at her, and replied, "He was up for the Medal of Honor, but they decided to recognize him with a Certificate of Merit instead..."

Polly quickly asked, "You hadn't given them the results of your investigation yet? Cuz still doesn't know he's innocent, does he? Is this final?"

With another sigh, the captain indicated that the telegram made it seem like the decision was final.

Lavinia entered the room and asked, "Why all the long faces?"

Polly quickly explained what the telegram had said. Before she could expound further, Lavinia assumed a stern expression and said, "Does get'n this Certificate of Merit instead of a Medal of Honor diminish Cuz's heroism?"

The captain started to explain, but was cut off as Lavinia continued, "So he gets a piece of paper rather than a medal for his uniform. Does that mean he saved any fewer lives? Does that mean he braved any fewer enemy bullets than he did? Whatever you give Cuz now won't change the appreciation and admiration the men he saved have for him. What he did was heroic and inspiring no matter what the Army says or does at this point."

Quickly looking over to Polly, he smiled and admitted that Lavinia was correct. He added, "Maybe one day the Army will create different medals to recognize such distinguished service. For now, though, being awarded the Certificate of Merit is a great honor, and I sincerely hope Cuz knows how much we all believe he deserves it."

Polly smiled as she quickly replied, "I believe he'll be too happy about learning he's not a murderer to care much about what recognition the Army gives him."

The captain tilted his head slightly as he expressed doubt. "I'm not sure Cuz will be exuberant over what I have discovered regarding Stumpy's death." Seeing the puzzled looks on both Polly's and her mother's faces, he explained, "I believe Cuz will be confused and perhaps frustrated. He may even become agitated and annoyed. Ask yourself what is the stronger emotion: realizing you are not guilty of a murder, or that you wasted your life trying to compensate for something you didn't do?"

The three stood silent for a moment as they considered the question. Breaking the silence, Lavinia barked, "Could've—would've—should've! All this worrying about what might've been ain't gonna get supper ready! Come on, Polly, give me a hand."

The following morning, the captain's morning coffee was interrupted as Polly and Lavinia barged into the kitchen and demanded to know why he wasn't ready to go yet. With a confused look, he asked politely what the ladies were talking about.

With her hands on her hips, Polly stated, "The family tradition I told you about!"

The captain looked like a lost rabbit being cornered.

She continued, "This is Saturday, the day between Good Friday and Easter Sunday. This is the day our family always goes to the cemetery and pays our respects to our deceased loved ones."

Pretending to have remembered being told about this family tradition, he asked for their forgiveness and promised to be ready in just a couple of minutes. As he left the room, he could hear Lavinia quietly mumble, "Men— honestly!"

Once ready, he hurried to find Polly and her mother in the back garden picking flowers to take with them. This gave him an idea, so he asked, "Mrs. Reiley, do you think we can collect about 50 more flowers?"

She shot Polly an annoyed look, not because of the request but that he continued to call her "Mrs. Reiley."

Facing her son-in-law and without concern as to why he would need so many flowers, she replied, "Daniel, if you ask me politely and call me Lavinia, I'll find you 50 flowers!"

Clearing his throat and giving an embarrassed look towards his wife, he asked, "Lavinia, can you please help me collect 50 flowers before we go to the cemetery?"

With a squeal of victory, she gave her son-in-law a big hug and promised to help him with his flower quest.

After some light bartering with a couple of the neighbors, they were able to collect the necessary flowers for their journey. The three talked and reminisced over past family times and former family customs. As they pulled into Calvary Cemetery, Polly asked, "Where are we? We're not where I thought we'd be heading."

The captain explained, "Cuz's parents are buried here. I want to leave flowers on Cuz's behalf."

Within minutes, they located the marker for Austina Hayes, Cuz's mother, who had died in November of 1868. On one side of Austina were her parents. Her mother had died only a year before and was one of the first to be buried in Calvary. Austina's father died about a year after her murder. On the other side of Austina's grave was the marker for Christopher Hayes who died nearly 10 years after she did.

Lavinia pulled some grass back from the markers and brushed some leaves away as she made room for the captain to place a couple of flowers. Polly brushed some dirt off of the marker. Quietly, they made their way out of the cemetery.

The next stop was Elmwood Cemetery. Lavinia led them directly to her parents' graves. After some cleaning and trimming, she told a couple of stories about her memories of them. Polly led the way to a nearby section where her father was buried a short distance away from her paternal grandparents. Again, they cleaned, trimmed, and reflected on their memories.

With the assistance of one of the cemetery workers, they made their way to the section of Elmwood known as "No Man's Land." Here, over 2,500 victims of the yellow fever epidemics were buried in mass trenches. During the height of the epidemic, as many as 50 burials a day occurred in the trenches. While they may have had varied positions in the community—lawyers, doctors, preachers, prostitutes, merchants, and laborers—they were all laid to rest side-by-side in these mass burial lots.

Walking between two of the four spaces, the captain stopped and placed a flower on the ground in honor of Suzanne Dugan who was more affectionately referred to as "Miss Suzy." She had died in the summer of 1879 and therefore buried in the last of the four yellow fever mass trenches. He stood and quietly thought of the sacrifices and heroics of many of the citizens during the various epidemics.

With several flowers remaining, Polly and Lavinia knew they had at least one more stop to make. Pulling up to St. Agnes, the captain gathered the remaining flowers and escorted his wife and Lavinia to the small cemetery hidden behind a hedgerow. Here were several markers for nuns and priests who had died while caring for victims of the yellow death. The captain explained, "Thirty sisters and 16 priests perished while selflessly caring for others."

There was no cleaning or trimming necessary for these markers. The nuns of St. Agnes kept each resting place neat and orderly. Slowly and respectfully, they placed a flower on each yellow fever victim's grave. Polly and Lavinia took turns reading the names off the marker as they placed each flower.

Two nuns appeared and watched as the captain placed the final two flowers. Looking up after placing the last one, he noticed that one of the nuns was Sister Margarete. He quickly made the introductions as she started to say the flowers were appreciated yet unnecessary.

Lavinia said, "It was worth it just to get him to call me by my name!"

Politely, Sister Margarete smiled even though she had no idea what Lavinia was talking about.

The captain quickly changed the subject. "I'm very happy I got to see you before we left town. I wanted to let you know that I was able to prove that Gunsie didn't kill Clarence Green Vendig. Also, I just heard yesterday that even though he will not be receiving the Medal of Honor, he will be receiving a Certificate of Merit for his actions in Cuba."

Sister Margarete and the captain spoke about his other findings from his investigation. Eventually, the other sister respectfully reminded Sister Margarete of the time. She then apologized for having to run off and again thanked them for the flowers and the update on Gunsie.

On Easter Sunday, the captain, Polly, and Lavinia attended church services at Calvary Episcopal Church. As they took their seats, the captain spotted a couple of familiar faces. First, there was Frank Mann, the desk sergeant who recorded Austina's death and provided so much valuable information to the captain in the early stages of his investigation. Next, he noticed Eli across the sanctuary being friendly to an apparent widow who was close to his age. Looking towards the back of the chapel, the captain was surprised to make eye contact with Miss Cynthia from the brothel. She smiled mischievously and winked before motioning her hand in a manner that resembled a tiger pawing for food.

As the service began to get underway, a young lady quickly plopped down beside the captain. It was J.B. Her parents scurried up to sit as they tried to understand why she had run to sit by this man. J.B. didn't make eye contact with the captain, but did reach down to touch the leather of his boot once. When it came time to sing, J.B. didn't use a hymnal but managed to sing like an angel nonetheless.

After the service, J.B. ran off without saying a word. The captain glanced towards the back and again received a wink from Miss Cynthia.

Interrupting his embarrassment, he heard his name called out as Eli walked over to greet him and his family. "Captain Hodge, you look rather flustered. Are you all right?"

Quickly composing himself after again seeing his winking admirer, he replied, "Yes, I'm doing quite well. Wonderful sermon this morning—very stirring."

Lavinia added, "Reverend Davenport always delivers an inspirational and enlightening sermon, don't you think so?"

Eli heartily agreed as he then expressed his happiness at seeing the captain and Polly before they left town. "It's going to be rather dull around here without you kicking the dust off of 17-year old stories."

After a good laugh and some more quips, the captain dug into his pocket and pulled out a piece of paper that he handed to Eli. "Here are the names of two doctors at the John Hopkins University in Maryland. These men are researching savants and their unique abilities. They may be able to help J.B. with her social interaction skills."

Eli smiled and thanked him. "I'll make sure her parents get this."

A man and a woman walked up and greeted Eli. Eli looked happy to see them. "Robert! How are you and your family?"

The man introduced his wife to Eli. Eli then introduced him to the captain, Polly, and Lavinia. "Robert McLean is the vice president of the William R. Moore Dry Goods Company." Eli turned to face the captain directly as he asked, "Do you remember me talking about my high hopes for this town's future? Well, this man kindled most of that hope."

Robert shrugged off the compliment as he said, "Nonsense. You give me too much credit. However, there is a young man I know who talks about a very bright future for Memphis. He may be just the man to make it a reality."

Robert turned and waved a young couple over. As they arrived, Robert said, "This is my daughter Bessie..."

She politely interjected, "Please call me Betty."

Robert and his wife both chuckled lightly at her correction before he continued. "This young man with her is Mr. Edward H. Crump. I'm telling you truthfully, after talking to this young man for an hour, you'll know that he's going to put Memphis on the map!"

The captain asked, "What is it that you do, Mr. Crump?"

"I work for the Walter Goodman Cotton Company over on Front Street. I'm learning about the cotton business by being a broker and trader."

Eli was intrigued and started asking Edward more specific questions about his vision for Memphis when Mrs. McLean leaned towards the captain and quietly said, "I think that woman over there is trying to get your attention."

His fear was confirmed as he glanced towards the back of the sanctuary—it was Miss Cynthia motioning for him to come towards her.

Polly muttered, "Honestly, Daniel! Haven't you had enough of the painted ladies for one trip to Memphis?"

Mrs. McLean and Lavinia shared a startled expression as Polly uncomfortably realized how her comment sounded. Eli, Robert, and Edward were too busy talking to overhear what she had said.

The captain politely excused himself from the group as he walked over to find out what Miss Cynthia needed to tell him. As he walked away, Mrs. McLean and Lavinia looked at Polly inquisitively. Polly smiled and said, "It's all right—he's a doctor."

Walking closer to Miss Cynthia, the captain saw her mischievous smile grow as she said, "Well, hello, tiger!"

"Hello, Miss Cynthia. I take it that there was something you needed to tell me?"

After a prolonged smile, she said, "You know, I should be very upset with you."

"Oh, really? What did I do to upset you?"

She sighed deeply as she looked him over before replying. "You cost me one of my best girls. After your visit, Cairy packed up and left. But seeing as how she was running off to be with her man, I guess I can understand."

With a puzzled look, he asked, "She ran off to be with her man?"

Miss Cynthia could see his wife watching, so she lightly stroked the captain's arm just to see Polly's reaction. As soon as Miss Cynthia saw Polly bristle, she laughed and then answered his question. "That boy named Cuz. She ran off to be with him."

The captain grinned broadly. In his excitement, he reached out and grabbed Miss Cynthia's upper arms as he exclaimed, "That's excellent news! Thank you very much for letting me know. I greatly appreciate it."

He quickly turned to walk back towards the others to share the news with them. As he walked away, Miss Cynthia started to tell him that he would always be welcome at her place, but decided that a church sanctuary probably wasn't the most ideal place for her to be soliciting for business.

When the captain returned to the others, he avoided dwelling on Polly's dismissive look and chose to engage in the ongoing discussion between Eli and Edward. Edward was envisioning the city's expansion to the north, east, and south, while Eli argued that the swamps and bayous surrounding the Wolf River and the Nonconnah Creek would restrict growth to the east exclusively.

Since the captain had no opinion on the matter, he announced they needed to leave and said their farewells. In parting, the captain shook Edward's hand and said, "It sounds like you have a good grasp on the city's needs. You should go into government administration in some capacity."

Edward gave a determined smile and said, "That is on my plan for the near future. Thank you for your confidence in me."

Lavinia smiled and interjected, "If you are going to run for political office, won't you need a wife by your side?"

Edward grinned and Betty blushed as they collectively attempted to change the subject. Her parents laughed at Lavinia's attempt to provoke a commitment from either one of the young adults. The laughter even seemed to mellow Polly's earlier moment of possessiveness.

As they all walked towards the exit, Lavinia invited them to Sunday dinner. However, they all had commitments elsewhere.

As the captain, Polly, and Lavinia made their way back to the house, he told them about Cairy going to be with Cuz. Polly said, "I wonder if Cuz and Cairy can adjust after their years of separation."

Lavinia optimistically said, "Well, they both have issues they want to forget, and they can help each other move forward."

After a lengthy pause, Polly asked her husband what he thought would happen with Cuz and Cairy after all these years. He just smiled and said, "They'll be fine. I really think they'll be good for one another."

The next morning, the captain and Polly were packed and ready to make their way back to their home. Sitting around the table after breakfast, the captain started to reflect on his visit. "Cuz and his friend Ira are true survivors. By the time they were teenagers, they had been surrounded by death brought on by the evil of man as well as by plague. To have lived in Memphis through the 1870s—and survived—well, that was quite an accomplishment in and of itself."

Lavinia agreed and added, "The city finally got its charter back and began to claw its way out of the mud and filth. New roads were made, clean water became plentiful, raw sewage no longer flowed out into the streets. Once we opened that new bridge to Arkansas, we started growing real steady with businesses eager to sell goods to all the westward-bound folk."

Polly jumped into the conversation by pointing out that with citizens like Edward Crump coming to live in Memphis, the future opportunities were limitless.

This prompted the captain to say, "Yes, Mr. Crump has some very expansive ideas as to how this city should develop, not to mention his own aggressive personal goals."

The knock on the front door signaled it was time to say their goodbyes. With a roll of the eyes, the captain took a deep breath and said, "Thank you very much for your hospitality, Lavinia. We greatly appreciate it."

With a big smile and a twinkle in her eye, she replied, "See? You can teach an old dog new tricks!"

Polly and her mother teared up as they were promising to write. Polly then said, "Tell that husband of yours that we are sorry we missed him."

The captain excitedly added, "Yes, tell George he needs to make a lot more of that red-currant wine."

Lavinia quipped, "For us or for the widows?"

In short time the captain and Polly were boarding the train for home. As they got situated, they noticed a commotion outside. Several policemen were rushing up to board the train. Two of them entered their car and started asking in a very authoritative voice, "Captain Daniel Hodge—please identify yourself. Is Captain Daniel Hodge onboard?"

The captain and his wife exchanged puzzled looks as the captain acknowledged who he was. While one officer asked that the captain remain in his seat, the other officer exited the car. The captain asked, "What is all this about?"

The policeman simply held his hand out as he said, "We were sent to find you."

The other passengers were becoming very suspicious as to why the captain and Polly were being singled out. Before they could ask any more questions, another policeman entered the front of the car. It was Sergeant Allen Vickery. While the captain started to smile and offer a friendly greeting, Sarge looked directly at Polly and said in a very official tone, "Ma'am, is this man attempting to take you away against your will?"

Polly was stunned and was trying to answer when Sarge started laughing and shook hands with the captain, who said, "You love to make an entrance, I see."

Sarge apologized to Polly for making her uncomfortable with his shenanigans. She just laughed it off. Sarge then said, "I heard you were leaving today and asked my wife to make you some cornbread for the road." He then presented them with a large bag.

The conductor was announcing the train's pending departure. Before he left, Sarge told them, "Please stop in when you return. My wife and I would love to have you both over for dinner. You can tell me how the story ends regarding your soldier friend."

The captain and Polly wished Sarge well and promised to visit on their next trip to Memphis.

After a couple of hours traveling, the captain took a bite of cornbread and made a drawn-out sound of approval. As he turned to tell Polly he wished they had some of George's wine, she showed him a bottle of elderberry wine. His eyes grew wide as Polly asked, "You got a way to get the cork out?"

Nearly choking on the cornbread, he exclaimed, "I'll find a way to get it open!"

Acknowledgements

I want to express my sincere appreciation for the knowledge, talent, and collaboration provided by my editor, Katherine Spivey of Alexandria, Virginia. She has been a tremendous partner throughout the process of writing my novels.

In addition, I have great admiration for the talent and insight of Soozie LaVelle Lowry of Manchester, Tennessee. She effortlessly transforms my cover art visions into reality. Thank you for your artistic skill and graphic interpretation. You can see more of her creations at her website: http://www.soozielowry.com

Staying in Touch

Readers can follow me at the following locations:

Facebook –
https://www.facebook.com/authorKeithKeltner/?ref=a
ymt_homepage_panel

Website –
http://www.shymur.net

Email –
keith.keltner@shymur.net

Linkedin –
https://www.linkedin.com/in/keith-keltner-5a428b1

Smashwords –
https://www.smashwords.com/profile/view/Shymur